A Harlequin Romance

OTHER

Harlequin Romances

by RUTH CLEMENCE

1195—SPREAD YOUR WINGS
1418—A CURE WITH KINDNESS
1619—HAPPY WITH EITHER
1697—HEALING IN THE HILLS
1814—A TIME TO LOVE

A TIME TO LOVE

by

RUTH CLEMENCE

HARLEQUIN BOOKS

TORONTO
WINNIPEG

Original hard cover edition published in 1974
by Mills & Boon Limited.

SBN 373-01814-2

Harlequin edition published September 1974

All the characters in this book have no existence outside the imagination of the Author, and have no relation whatsoever to anyone bearing the same name or names. They are not even distantly inspired by any individual known or unknown to the Author, and all the incidents are pure invention.

Printed in Canada

1814

CHAPTER 1

ANGELINA SNOW walked slowly across St. Mark's Square and thought longingly of the leisurely bath she would have on reaching her hotel, followed by a carefully chosen dinner at the little table in the corner of the dining room the head waiter always kept for her. It had been foolish on a humid afternoon like this to join the party of sightseers on a trip to the glass factory on the island of Murano, but whenever she visited Venice Angie was invariably drawn back to see the beautiful fragile Venetian glass being made, and to-day she had been lured into doing so by the promise of a cool sail in the motorboat across the lagoon.

It had been anything but cool, however, when she and the other tourists entered the interior of the factory, and since this was meant to be a convalescent holiday after a particularly vicious attack of 'flu, it had been the height of foolishness to give in to her curiosity to see the glass-blowers at work again.

But at least she had one good thing to show for her imprudence, Angie mused. The problem of a wedding gift for her secretary, Audrey Wood, who was getting married in July, was now solved. Although it meant she would have to carry an extra parcel all the way back to England, Angie had been unable to resist a set of wine goblets with a vine leaf design which had been on show in the factory display shop, and now a cardboard box hung from her arm as she walked back to her hotel.

She leaned wearily against the wall as the lift carried her up to her floor. Now that Aunt Pam and Uncle Luigi had moved to Sardinia and the old palazzo where she and her sister had spent many happy school holidays had been sold, Angelina stayed at a hotel when she visited her beloved Venice. She had come at least once a year since the age of seven, at first with her father, mother and sister Robinetta, but since Uncle Luigi's retirement and her parents' death in a car accident, alone here at the same comfortable hotel in the old part of the city.

As Angie turned the key in her bedroom door she was startled by the sound of weeping, and had hardly pushed the door ajar before her sister impetuously flung herself into Angelina's arms. 'Heavens, Netta!' Quickly Angie deposited her precious parcel and handbag on to a handy chair and leading the weeping girl over to one of the twin beds, persuaded her to sit down and handing her a clean tissue asked, 'What brings you here? Not good news, I can see.'

Angie smiled, but no answering smile appeared on the delicate features of her younger sister. There was little similarity between the girls. Robinetta Snow was a typical English rose; curling blonde hair, big grey eyes with long sweeping lashes, a flawless complexion and a figure that impinged upon even the most jaded masculine appetite. Angie on the other hand was small and plain by comparison. She had soon discovered that only clever make-up and dress would save her from being completely overlooked, and had made it her business to find out what suited her at the age of eighteen and as far as fashion permitted stuck to her own style and colours so that over the years she had built up a reputation for being chic.

Angie sighed inwardly as she asked again, 'Come on, Netta, you may as well tell me what's troubling you. I don't suppose you've come all the way to Italy just to tell me you've broken a fingernail or caught a bad cold. I thought you were busy just now on that soap assignment.'

'Oh, Angie, I wish I were dead! I know you're here to get over 'flu and truly I didn't want to bother you, but when Pablo said I'd been imagining the whole thing and he'd never had any intention of marrying me I just had to talk to you. What am I going to do? I've told everyone; in fact I'd started ordering things for an engagement party, and Pablo says it's all off. I love him so. How can he treat me like this? Now he's not even in London, or so that horrid man Steve Wells tells me, though I think Pablo just won't speak to me. I even went round to the studio late at night, but no one answered. He must have seen me coming and refused to answer the bell. Tell me what I'm to do. It can't end like this!'

Robinetta took the tissue Angie was holding out to her and delicately blew her nose, then getting up she peered anxiously into the mirror to inspect the damage her tears had left behind. Watching her sister Angelina noted that there was scarcely a mark on the perfect features. To anyone else the involved explanation would have meant nothing, but Angie was used to Robinetta's rambling sentences. Sighing, she kicked off her shoes. 'What good is it asking my advice? You've been formally engaged three times since you were seventeen and I've lost track of the number of men lining up to become Mr. Robinetta Snow. What has this Pablo got that the others haven't? Oh, I know you've been seeing a fair bit of him, but then you've been working together on these advertising campaigns some time now, haven't you? When will you learn that business and pleasure don't mix?'

'It's all very well for you to talk,' Robinetta swung round from the mirror. 'You don't have a glamour-boy for a boss. Not that you'd notice if you did.'

A silence followed these spiteful words. Angie walked into the bathroom and turned on the bath taps. By the time she returned she was unzipping her slacks and shedding the rest of her clothes to pull on a lightweight dressing-gown. She stopped a second to glance at Netta, who was eyeing her defiantly. 'I thought we were discussing your entanglements, not my personal life,' Angie said at last quietly. 'In any case, Basil may seem dull to you, but he's a very decent bloke. He's happily married and doesn't look at anyone else except Babs.'

Basil Beavis had been Angie's boss for the last three years. He was editor of the women's magazine on which she worked and it had been he who had insisted that Angie have a break after her illness. 'We're nearly through the series now, it would be a pity to spoil it by your last articles ending on a sour, uninteresting note. Get away before you interview your next celebrity or you'll be looking at him with very jaundiced eyes indeed in your present state,' he had concluded shrewdly as he glanced at Angie's pale face across the desk, and taking him at his word, Angie had booked a ticket and flown out to Venice the following day. A short break after the grind of the last few months would be a godsend.

As Angie opened the wardrobe to get out a dress Netta said, 'Don't be long in the bathroom. I'm absolutely filthy after that plane journey and I'm dying for a bath myself.' Typically Netta, Angie thought as she closed the bathroom door behind her, and taking off her robe stepped into the hot perfumed water. Her sister must have arrived some time before she herself returned from the glass factory. She could have taken three or four baths and yet she had waited to pour out all her troubles and then, her mind clear, demand priority in the bathroom. It's lucky for her I always book a double room, Angie thought, still resentful at Netta's demand. She had found from experience, however, that single rooms in continental hotels were not only hard to come by but often very cramped and in a disagreeable part of the hotel, frequently within sound and smell of the kitchen or overlooking a main road.

Of course in Venice most of the hotels looked over the canals. Angie's own bedroom balcony projected over one of the smaller canals and she had had her breakfast there every morning so far, glorying in the view from her window and in the gondolas passing beneath.

As she soaped herself Angie wondered what she was going to do about solving Robinetta's latest romantic tangle. It had been like this ever since their parents were killed five years ago. Angie had just finished her final examinations at university and was awaiting the results, and Robinetta at boarding school had just taken her 'O' levels when Angela and Robin Snow, on their way to visit friends in Scotland, had been killed simultaneously in a pile-up on the motorway. Their father's younger brother John had come home from the Far East to help straighten things out for the girls. He had been named as one of the trustees in Robin Snow's will, and with the help of the family solicitor had stayed long enough to sort things out before he returned to his job as foreign correspondent.

During his brief stay in England John Snow had discovered that Angie herself had a leaning towards journalism and he had helped her get a position on one of the popular weekly magazines. 'No good trying to become a newspaper woman. It's too tough a business for a girl like you,' he had advised her. 'Not that I'd recommend it to any woman.' He had looked so like her father that Angie had almost cried. 'Now if you go on to the staff of a woman's magazine, although you'll have to work hard, the climate isn't quite the same.'

Certainly Angie had been very happy in the job her Uncle John had found her. She had stayed there almost two years, working in almost every department of the magazine, mostly at everyone's beck and call. But she had not minded; it had been good experience, and when a position had been advertised on a very glossy monthly, she had promptly applied for the job and had been fortunate enough to get it.

Angelina had admitted to herself, though, that it probably wouldn't have been so easy without the influence of her old friend James Stanscombe, and during the first few weeks she had sensed an atmosphere of animosity from the rest of the staff. But they soon realised Angie had no intention of taking advantage of the fact that she was on Christian-name terms with the editor, Basil Beavis, James's old school friend, and that she was prepared to tackle anything which landed on her desk and if necessary work long hours into the bargain.

She had been delighted when ten months earlier this hard work had paid off and Basil picked her to do a special series of articles on men famous in their particular spheres. Angie had discovered rather to her own surprise that she was an adept interviewer. Something about her manner seemed to induce people to confide in her; details flowed from them about their private life, their ambitions and innermost thoughts which they would have thought twice about telling almost anybody else. Perhaps the fact that she was not a pretty, 'dolly' girl helped, and her quiet unassuming manner might have had something to do with her success as well.

Basil Beavis had given her a good research team, but she had had to work very hard to make the articles interesting and informative without appearing sensational. So far she had interviewed nine well-known personalities and she still had three more to see before the series was completed. Her behind-the-scenes glimpses of a famous film actor, a racing driver, one of the leading avant-garde dressmakers, a ballet dancer, a young member of the aristocracy, a Nobel prizewinner and a boxer, a hairdresser who had revolutionalised women's hair-styles as well as a prominent M.P. had increased sales considerably. When she got back to England Angie knew she was to interview the man whose name had been on her sister's lips only a few minutes before—Pablo Pendleton, the photographer. Should she tell Robinetta that her next assignment was the man whom Netta alleged had led her on to think he intended to marry her? Pablo Pendleton was renowned for his refusal to give interviews to the Press, and Basil had had some difficulty in persuading him to make an exception in their case, and to permit Angie to move in and see him.

For these interviews could not be completed in a day but often took as long as a week. She usually had to spend several days in and around the V.I.P.'s home so she could get inside their skins and study each facet of their character, see them day by day going about their work, for honest details were what appealed to the readers.

So far nobody had objected to Angie's methods. Even the young duke had seemed rather flattered by all the fuss which had been made when his interview came up, and had thrown open his stately home even to the private apartments so that Angie and her photographer, Jack Bryant, could wander around at will. Jack was a character in himself. He had been a newspaper photographer before he joined the staff of *Ladies' Graces* and he took his young wife, Sylvia, and their children Rupert and Emma with him whenever possible when he had to travel far afield as he disliked being parted from his family for long. He'd be at home when they interviewed Pablo Pendleton, Angie thought as she reluctantly got out of the bath, for Pablo had his studio in London.

And then she remembered that Netta had said she received no answer when she called. Of course, if Netta had been making a nuisance of herself it was possible, as she had admitted, that her knocking had been deliberately ignored. What sort of a man could Pablo be, Angie thought, to behave so disagreeably? Despite long experience of Robinetta's many impulsive love affairs, she began to frown at the thought that this particular man had spurned her young sister. Netta might be irritating in many ways, but she could be endearing when she chose and while, like their mother, she was not over-endowed with brains, at least her beauty more than made up for this lack of intelligence.

Angela Snow had been almost a double of her younger

daughter. The same huge grey eyes, the flawless complexion and golden hair, which even when she died at the age of forty-two had shown no thread of silver. It had been Angela Snow's whimsical idea to give her two daughters flamboyant derivations of her own and her husband's christian names.

Angie peeled on tights and slipping into her dressing-gown opened the bathroom door and went back into the bedroom. Her sister had by this time unpacked and was waiting rather impatiently to use the bathroom. 'I was wondering how much longer you were going to be,' she said. 'You've been simply ages.'

Angie didn't reply immediately as she walked over to the dressing-table. As she began to smooth her nails with an emery board she caught her sister's eye in the mirror. 'Well, it's all yours now,' she said, and smiled. 'You'll feel better when you've had a bath and we'll have some wine with dinner. The chef's rather good here.'

'I'm not hungry,' was Netta's parting shot as she closed the bathroom door, and Angie sighed once again as she began to make up her face. She could see that the last few days of her holiday were not going to be the placid uninterrupted restful ones which had gone before.

There had never been any question of Robinetta following Angie's example and going to university. After their parents' death she had flatly refused to go back to school and sit for her 'O' levels again, most of which she had failed to pass. On the advice of the trustees the big family house had been sold, their father's business had been bought out by a larger concern and Angie and the sixteen-year-old Robinetta had gone to London, where the two girls, their money safely invested, soon found a comfortable flat overlooking Regent's Park with an elderly housekeeper living in to do the housework and see to their meals.

There had been a family conference to decide what

Robinetta should do, since she refused vehemently to attend any school of further education. The choice had finally narrowed down to either an acting career or an attempt to become a model and Robinetta herself settled this point by failing the interview for drama school. John Snow had finally managed to get his niece's name down for one of the leading model agencies and Robinetta had spent twelve months training there before taking up her first professional appointment.

It had come as no surprise to Angelina that her younger sister had been an instant success. Before six months were up photographers were vying with one another for her services and her fee per hour had risen astronomically from a modest first beginning. Not only did Robinetta look extremely beautiful from any angle but she was also very photogenic, a much more important consideration to commercial photographers. Angelina was secretly of the opinion that if you put Netta into a piece of sackcloth and tied it round her waist with string she would still make it look like a model dress from one of the leading fashion houses.

During the following years while Angie steadily worked her way up the ladder at *Ladies' Graces*, the flat where the Snow sisters lived became a centre for a crowd of young people, mostly Robinetta's friends and acquaintances. Angie lost count of the stream of young men who came to escort her sister and stayed around for a while, then disappeared from the scene completely. Some had lasted longer than others; one or two had even managed to put an engagement ring on the third finger of Robinetta's left hand, but no one as yet had got her to the altar.

As time went on, Angelina began to dream of the day when Netta became someone else's responsibility, and she would no longer have to spend sleepless nights trying to sort out her sister's everlasting entanglements or in wondering the best way to deal with Netta's latest whim. Looking at her sister now as she waited for her to finish dressing, it was hard to imagine that this beautiful creature could be such a problem child. Angelina's mother had often been unconventional and unpredictable, but with a husband and two children to think about she had not had time to be flighty, and Angie would have given a great deal to have been able to confide her fears about Netta's instability of character to someone with more experience than herself.

But with Uncle John in Hongkong, Aunt Pam and Uncle Luigi in Sardinia, there remained only Aunt Helen, her mother's elder sister, the last person from whom Angie could seek advice. Aunt Helen was old-fashioned enough to disapprove of her nieces living on their own with only Mrs. Wilkinson's presence as a 'sop to propriety.' John Snow had laughed when Helen had come out with this outmoded phrase, but his assurance that everyone lived their own lives these days had done nothing to alter Aunt Helen's opinion, Angie remembered. If only Uncle John were not so far away and she could tell him about Netta's latest and most serious infatuation, but as she watched her sister carefully applying her make-up, Angie knew she would in the end have to sort it out unaided.

Odd though that her next interview when she returned to London was almost certainly with the man apparently occupying all Netta's thoughts. Already, despite the doubts Angie felt about the precise truth of her sister's story, she was beginning to feel prejudiced against Pablo Pendleton. Netta was a heavy responsibility, but after all she was her sister, and when it came to the crunch she would back her to the hilt. Angie could no more leave Robinetta to sink or swim alone than she could have flown.

By the time Robinetta Snow considered herself ready to face the public rooms in the hotel it was some half an hour later, and during the complicated process of putting on her make-up and doing her hair she had regaled Angie with many details of the 'affair Pendleton.' Eventually, satisfied at last with her appearance, Robinetta turned from the mirror to face her sister. 'Will I do?' she asked Angie, completely confident of an affirmative answer.

Angie's eyes surveyed the elegant figure. Robinetta was wearing a leaf green silk jersey dress, over which she had slipped a sleeveless jacket covered in glittering black sequins. On almost anyone else it might have looked too theatrical, but on Robinetta it looked perfect. It made Angie's brown silk trouser suit with the golden yellow chiffon blouse look very ordinary by comparison, and yet, until that moment, she had felt pleased with her appearance. Even the glimpse she saw in the long mirror of her brown hair brushed into a shining cap round her well-shaped head and the delicate gold filigree ear-rings which James Stanscombe had given her did nothing to make Angie feel anything but a very small brown mouse beside her breathtakingly glamorous sister.

She picked up her evening purse and led the way to the door. 'As you well know, Netta, you look marvellous. Now if you don't mind, let's go and eat, it's getting late.'

When the girls reached the dining room they were soon spotted by the head waiter. Since she had come to the hotel he had always placed Angie at a small table against the wall, and though he and the other waiters had always been helpful and attentive she smiled inwardly at the sudden buzz of activity which began around them when the dining-room staff discovered that she and Netta were together. No small unobtrusive table this evening, but one where everyone could see them, and although the service in this hotel was always good, to-night, with Netta at the table, it was outstanding.

Not that Robinetta ever appeared to notice the attention which her appearance aroused. She seemed to take it as her due that waiters would spring instantly to attention when she appeared and that her smallest wish was their command. She continued to talk interminably through the many courses about Pablo, about the soap ad on which they had been working together, about how much time she had spend in his studio, how many times he had taken her to dinner and how incomprehensible was his sudden change of heart. She repeatedly asked Angie for advice and then chattered on without waiting for a reply.

By the time they had reached the coffee stage Angie was feeling distinctly weary of Pablo Pendleton's name and wished she could send a cable to Basil Beavis asking him to let her interview anybody but this seemingly obnoxious man at present giving her sister so much heartache.

Apart from a bout of tears, however, as she was getting ready for bed, tired out by the journey and her own emotions, to Angelina's great relief by the following morning, Robinetta seemed to have talked herself out on the subject of her latest love affair. During their breakfast of delicious coffee and hot rolls spread lavishly with butter and black cherry jam, Robinetta seemed almost cheerful. She was even willing to fall in with Angelina's suggestion that instead of spending the day in Venice they should take a waterbus and visit the island of Torcello. Angelina knew that if they stayed in the town Robinetta would only want to look at the goods on display, and she didn't fancy a day walking the hot streets window-shopping.

It looked like being a nice day and it would be interesting to see the old church on the island which, Angelina recalled, had some beautiful frescoes. Some years earlier on a visit to Aunt Pam and Uncle Luigi, she had been taken there. It took Angelina some time to persuade Robinetta to leave the sunny balcony and wash and dress in a cotton outfit, apply only a minimum of make-up and tie her hair back for coolness with a chiffon scarf, but eventually she was ready and the two girls strolled down to the Fondamenta Nuova to board the boat for the trip out to Torcello. They landed forty-five minutes later at a small wooden quay and walked through a beautiful garden with wooden arches covered in climbing roses to see the church. By lunchtime they were hungry enough to welcome a visit to the restaurant where they could sit out of doors and their lunch of spit-roasted chicken was eaten in the shade of an old trellis covered with a climbing vine.

By mid-afternoon Robinetta tired of the island. No great admirer of nature, she was beginning to get fretful, and Angie lost no time in getting the boat back to Venice before there was another repetition of last night's bout of weeping self-pity. Something would have to be done about Robinetta's latest heartbreak, she could see.

'Have you got another commercial to do soon?' Angelina asked as they were returning to the hotel.

'No.' Robinetta kicked at a pebble with a small sandalled foot. 'At least, there were several, but I refused them all,' she added sullenly as the girls walked into the foyer of the hotel and went to collect their room key.

The lift was moving before Angie ventured, 'Wouldn't it be a good idea to go back to London with me on Friday and get on with some new work? You'd maybe find you'd blown up the situation out of all proportion.'

Robinetta was standing with bent head and did not answer. Then she looked up and her huge limpid eyes were full of tears. 'It's easy for you, Angie. You've never really been in love. I can't help it. I know I'm easily infatuated, but this time I'm sure it's the real thing at last.'

She was so obviously making a determined effort to control her tears that Angelina couldn't resist putting an arm round her sister's shoulders and giving her a squeeze. This was the side of Netta which inevitably melted her heart. 'Well, if you don't feel like going back immediately,' she went on as they walked along the corridor towards their room, 'why don't you fly down to Sardinia for a few days? You know if we give Aunt Pam a ring she'll be only too happy to see you. I think she was a bit hurt that I didn't go there myself this holiday, but I felt I wanted to be on my own.'

When the bedroom door was open Robinetta walked across and dropped her handbag on to the bed. She sat down, slipped off her sandals and stretching out her feet regarded them pensively for a moment before she looked up. 'It mightn't be a bad idea,' she agreed, and then suddenly and impetuously rushed on, 'I'm truly sorry, Angie. I quite forgot you were here because you'd been ill. I just phoned Heathrow for a booking and came rushing out as soon as I got in a state over Pablo's beastly behaviour. I never think first, do I? I had no right to interrupt your sick leave,' she finished, but before a surprised Angelina could reply to the unexpected apology, Robinetta had turned to pick up the telephone.

Both girls had been coming to Venice on visits for so many years they were fairly fluent in Italian and Robinetta had no trouble in getting herself connected with her aunt's number in Sardinia. The girls' younger maternal aunt had married an impoverished Italian nobleman much against her parents' wishes, but despite their disapproval, the marriage had been an ideally happy one. It only required a brief explanation of her predicament and within a few minutes Aunt Pam was assuring Robinetta that she could come and stay as long as she wished, soak up the sun and forget her heartaches. Angie had a brief word too before the call ended, apologising for being unable to visit the island this time and promising to ring again as soon as she arrived back in England.

Robinetta gave a satisfied smile as Angie replaced the receiver. 'That was a brilliant idea. I'll be able to ask Pam for advice; she's always so understanding. She was always ready to help even when we were kids. She's bound to know what I ought to do.'

Angie sighed to herself as she nodded and turned away. Netta was right, Pam was the sympathetic one of the family, and it seemed mean to send her sister off to weep over her grievances on someone else's shoulder, particularly when that shoulder belonged to her favourite aunt. Aunt Helen, her mother's other sister, ought to have been the one to whom they could turn, but she disapproved so strongly of the actions of the younger generation and, it seemed, her two nieces in particular, that she was the last person to go to when in difficulty. She thought it her duty to visit them at frequent intervals, but always for the purpose of criticising, it seemed to Angelina. Helen Pitman's most constant remark was, 'Modern girls, I'll never understand them,' and since she made no effort to see their point of view, it was unlikely she ever would.

Angie bore Aunt Helen's visits with patience, but Robinetta was inclined to fret at the carping remarks and never failed to speak her mind as soon as the unwelcome guest had departed. No sisters could be more different, Angie thought as she got ready for bed. Pam, the willing, warm-hearted one, the one to whom they invariably turned as children, was once again being called upon to offer assistance.

The following lunchtime Robinetta departed for Sardinia already looking a good deal more cheerful at the prospect of unburdening herself once again to an accommodating listener. As the plane disappeared from sight, Angelina left the airport observatory balcony and decided to make the most of her last day here before she too packed and caught her flight to London. The sun shone from a clear blue sky and she stayed out until a combination of hunger and fatigue made her return for a last visit to the dining room to have her favourite Italian dishes, and an early night during which she slept deeply and dreamlessly.

Too soon she was back in the flat she shared with Robinetta, and being greeted by Mrs. Wilkinson. Once again she thought what a blessing it was they had the means to pay a full-time housekeeper, for Angie knew she would never have been able to cope with Netta's untidiness unaided. Mrs. Wilkinson was a widow, a Londoner by birth, and thoroughly enjoyed her comfortable position looking after the domestic arrangements for two easy-going girls, both prepared to turn a blind eye to the size of the housekeeping bills. Fortunately the sale of the big old family house on the Thames and their father's business had left them comfortably provided for without the addition of the salaries from their lucrative jobs. They were also fortunate that through her modelling Robinetta was often able to get expensive clothes for both herself and her sister at much reduced rates. It enabled them to indulge in luxuries other girls could not afford.

When Angie arrived in her office the following Monday morning there was a note propped against the telephone with a message that the editor wished to see her as soon as she arrived. She spoke on the intercom to his secretary and discovered that Basil Beavis was already in, and when a few minutes later Angie strolled into his office he looked up and smiled. 'Had a good rest, Angie my dear? You're looking a thousand times better than when you left. You looked to be going downhill fast.'

Angie laughed as she put a small package on the desk in front of Basil. 'Glad you think I'm back to normal! I couldn't resist getting this for you.' She nodded at the parcel. 'Now don't say I shouldn't have brought you anything back,' and she smiled her rather captivating smile as he looked up.

Basil slowly unwrapped the beautiful cut glass tankard which Angie had spotted in a shop the day before she left Venice. It had been made in the factory where she had bought the glass for her secretary's wedding present, but had passed unnoticed when she inspected the enormous display of glassware glittering like Aladdin's cave.

'I didn't bring anything for Babs,' Angie apologised as Basil held the tankard up to the light to catch the sunshine coming through the window behind him.

'Don't worry,' Basil advised her. 'Babs gets all the surprises as a rule. Thanks, my dear,' then coming abruptly to the business in hand, he went on, 'Good thing in a way you've been on holiday. I had to pull out all the stops, as you know, to fix up an interview with Pablo Pendleton, and I got a letter a week ago saying he can't see you in London after all and unless you and Jack go down to his place in Wales the whole business is off. Now I don't want to scrap it because the other two interviews can't be fitted in this month. I tried to arrange for you to see Stuart Blair instead, but he's filming abroad right now and that young barrister that you're interviewing as your last V.I.P. is on holiday at the moment, so it's got to be Pablo Pendleton or nobody. I've said of course you'd be quite willing to go to Wales and I've booked you in at the local pub. Jack's taking his caravan with the family, so he won't want to stay there too, but I daresay he'll be dropping in from time to time,' and Basil laughed and made a gesture of lifting a glass. Jack Bryant was the magazine's top photographer but famous in the business for his fondness for a glass of beer. Angie's mind was on a different tack, however.

'Where does the great man live?' she asked, and her tone was so tart that Basil gave her a keen glance as he replied.

'A small place called Llantarwyn. It's only over the Welsh border about forty miles from Ludlow. How will you get there? Going to drive yourself down?'

'I suppose I could,' Angie answered thoughtfully, 'though I'm not particularly keen on driving long distances on my own. I'm such a rotten navigator.'

'There's nothing to stop you going with Jack.'

'No. His kids are sweet, but two hundred miles cooped up with them is more than I could stand,' Angie laughed. 'I could go by train to Shrewsbury or Oswestry and Jack could meet me. What's Pendleton's home like? Worth photographing?'

'No idea,' Basil Beavis replied, and he pushed some papers across the desk to her. 'Here's all the information I've got to date. You'd better see Jack yourself and sort it out between you. I've provisionally said that you'll be down to see him on Wednesday or Thursday, but Pendleton's telephone number's there. Perhaps you'd like to ring up and fix it with the gentleman himself.'

'Or perhaps it would be better if I went down and took him by surprise,' Angelina said, and got to her feet, picking up the papers Basil had given her as she did so.

'Perhaps it would. I don't think he's going to be too easy a customer to deal with. However, do your best. I know you will in any case,' said Basil as Angie went towards the door.

She lost no time in seeking out Jack Bryant and they settled plans for getting to Wales. 'Sylvia's all ready. The caravan's stocked up. All I've got to do is hook up, load the family and take off,' Jack told Angie.

'Well, I suggest you do that to-morrow and then give me a ring at the flat when you've found a place to park and you've settled in. I've a bed at the local pub. Basil's already booked me in. And I've decided not to drive but to go by train—it will be less strain. Perhaps you could meet me in at the nearest railway station. Anyway, once you've found a decent camping site and given me a ring I'll have had time to check on possible trains.'

Jack departed after promising to ring as soon as he was fixed up and Angie spent the rest of the day with her research team, finding out from them how much they had managed to dig up about the publicity-shy Pablo Pendleton. Apart from the fact that he was half Spanish and half English, that most of his best work was the photographing of beautiful girls and that he had become famous only two years ago there was very little that they had been able to find out about him.

'I'm afraid you're going to have to start practically from

scratch,' Bruce Williams said to her as he handed over the folder containing the information the team had compiled. 'There are a few personal details there, of course, and we think we've discovered one important fact. He has a hobby quite apart from his usual commercial photography.'

'And what's that?' Angie enquired as she put the papers and a tape recorder into her briefcase.

'We haven't been able to find out for certain, but rumour says he paints, and quite proficiently too.'

'My goodness,' Angie laughed, 'this one's going to be a lulu! I've come across secret drinkers, but secret painters – wow!' She did not however explain that she had additional personal difficulties because of her sister's connection with her latest V.I.P. There was little doubt that Pablo Pendleton as soon as he discovered her surname would guess she was kin to Robinetta and Angie had no intention of lying to him. In any case, despite their dissimilarity in appearance, if he really wanted to find out it would take very little effort to discover Angie's near relationship with the beautiful model who had figured in so many of his commercial ventures.

Jack Bryant phoned up later that night to say that he, Sylvia and the children were happily settled in a farmer's field not three-quarters of a mile from Pablo Pendleton's house. 'I'm told it's quite a large place,' Jack went on. 'I imagine he doesn't live there alone, but I'm going into the pub now to do my big sleuthing act and see what I can find out about him. I'll meet you to-morrow afternoon. What time again did you say your train gets in?'

Angie repeated her expected time of arrival, and putting down the phone gazed thoughtfully at the instrument. She could see that this was going to be one of the most difficult interviews of her career and she wasn't looking forward to the prospect at all. Sighing, she got up, packed her suitcase and then made herself a hot drink and got into bed. Mrs. Wilkinson had gone out for the evening and she was alone in the flat. She wondered if she ought to ring James Stanscombe before she went off to Wales. But they had always had a very elastic relationship and she had already told him her plans.

James, long separated amicably from his wife and children, lived in a comfortable bachelor flat in Portman Square and he and Angelina had known one another for more than four years. They had been introduced in the first place by Angie's Uncle John, and they had seen one another frequently since that first meeting, usually for dinner in some quiet restaurant, or for a visit to the ballet or a concert.

James was an undemanding escort. Angie had the impression that he hardly needed the female of the species except as an occasional companion to stave off a surfeit of the bachelor life and often wondered why he had ever married in the first place. His comfortable flat was efficiently looked after by an elderly manservant who had been with him since he settled in London after he and his wife parted; she to continue to live in the family house in Essex and look after the children.

The weather had turned wet and cold and Angie packed plenty of warm clothes in anticipation of a miserably chilly week ahead. At the last moment she added two long dinner dresses to the contents of her suitcase. She might have no occasion to wear them, but they took up little room and being of uncrushable material would unpack without a wrinkle.

Next day, as soon as the train had left Euston, she took out the folder on Pablo Pendleton and went through its meagre contents yet again. Famous and well known though he now was as a photographer he seemed to be strangely reticent about his private life and was rarely photographed. The folder revealed little information about him, though there were plenty of photographs at the back of the folder. On top was the only reasonable print Angie's research team had been able to turn up of the elusive Mr. Pendleton himself, and even in this his face was half hidden by the coat collar of the glamorous-looking girl hanging on to his arm. The other photographs were glossy reproductions of Pablo Pendleton's more well-known advertising material, all of them commissioned by firms with famous brand names. Angie found herself looking at several in which her young sister figured, and as she reached the last photograph, she sat immobile for several long minutes staring down into Robinetta's smiling eyes.

There was a certain something in the expression of the eyes which Angie had never seen before. Her sister was staring straight at the camera, bending in a low-cut lacy negligée over a wash basin, her hands full of soapsuds cupped as if about to wash her face. Knowing Robinetta would cut off an arm sooner than put soap and water on her perfect skin, Angie smiled faintly as she put the photograph with the others and slid them back into the folder. Then she sat back and gazed sombrely through the window.

The idea of Netta washing her face might be amusing, but there was nothing to laugh at if that look in her eyes meant what Angelina thought it might imply. Her sister had never looked quite like that before. Perhaps she really wasn't exaggerating when she said Pablo Pendleton had led her up the garden path. Even Netta, impressionable though she was, wouldn't have allowed herself to go right overboard for any man without a lot of encouragement on his part. Not once during her previous engagements had Angie seen quite that look of loving tenderness on her sister's face. She had not perhaps exaggerated when she had confided to Angie in Venice that 'Pablo was special, someone one dreams all one's life of meeting.'

It was one thing for a plain Jane like herself to dream. Angie was popular among the men of her acquaintance and by no means a shrinking violet left sitting at home alone, but her men friends tended to treat her like one of the boys, and flowers and pretty compliments rarely came her way; more often it was a fraternal slap on the back. Strange therefore that Robinetta, beautiful, spoiled and attractive, should have secretly nursed a dream of a special Prince Charming of her own. Perhaps this was the real reason for her apparent inability to make a firm choice from among her many admirers and settle down.

Determinedly Angie dismissed the problem of her sister's latest love affair and her forthcoming interview with the man concerned from her mind and settled down to enjoy the journey. She had to change from the express to another train in Birmingham and from then on sat enraptured by the beauty of the countryside through which she was passing. All too soon her destination was reached and Angie passed the barrier to discover not only Jack Bryant but his pretty blonde wife Sylvia and their two small children all waiting to welcome her.

As soon as Jack had relieved her of her luggage the children lost no time in grabbing her by either hand. Angie had first met Jack and his family when she joined the staff of *Ladies' Graces* and by now she and the two well-behaved Bryant children were firm friends. They lost no time in telling Angie all about the caravan site. 'It's a lovely farm, Auntie Angie,' Rupert volunteered, 'and the farmer's got lots of chickens and two big fat pigs and a cow.'

'And the moo-cow's got a sweet little calf, Auntie Angie,' his younger sister broke in.

'Don't let them pester you,' Sylvia said, though she smiled indulgently at her two children as she spoke. You could tell from a glance how proud she was of the intelligent way in which both children conversed. Emma was not yet four, but already an age-old wisdom sat in her pretty blue eyes, and as she smiled up confidingly Angie found herself smiling back and squeezing the small fingers which lay within her own.

'Come on. Let's get in the car and you shall tell me more

about this farm.'

They needed no further encouragement, chattering uninhibitedly all the way to the local inn where Basil Beavis had booked Angie a room.

It transpired that Jack had arranged for them all to have an evening meal at the inn. 'Knowing you, we thought you'd probably have missed lunch and would be ready for an early dinner,' Sylvia said, 'so we've booked a table for seven o'clock. Then I can pop the children straight into bed when we get back to the caravan.'

'Give me time to wash and generally freshen up and I'll be right down,' Angie promised as she took the key from the receptionist and Jack carried her cases across the hall and up the stairs. It was only a modest establishment without even a porter to carry her luggage, but the bedroom, Angie discovered when she reached it, was comfortable and there was a fan heater set into the wall for the convenience of guests. She soon washed off the dirt of her journey and went downstairs again to join Jack and Sylvia who were busy restraining their youngsters from engaging every passing adult in conversation.

The five of them were soon seated round a small table in the dining room, as yet only patronised by two other couples. It was a jolly family meal and Angie found herself enjoying the cosy camaraderie which Jack and Sylvia enjoyed and the chatter of the two eager children.

Their table manners were really as exceptional as was their command of the English language, and Angie looked across the table at Sylvia with admiration. She could not imagine managing her own children so competently and most children she found over-indulged and precocious or pushed into the background to be 'seen but not heard.' Sylvia seemed to have hit a happy medium between. When it came time for her to raise a family Angie hoped she would be as wise.

As soon as the meal was over Jack and Sylvia got ready

to take the children back to the caravan. 'Everything set for the morning, is it?' Jack asked as they stood to say good-bye.

'Well, Basil said we were expected, but I think it might be a good idea if I rang and confirmed, don't you? Suppose you pick me up around nine?' Angie suggested. 'It may make a good impression if we arrive early.'

'Yes, and the light'll be better then,' Jack said, glancing up at the sky. 'I'd like to get some of the outside shots in the bag as early as possible. The weather forecast was sunny to-morrow. I may as well take the opportunity of getting the exteriors while the weather holds. Anyway, see you some time after nine,' and waving, he set off to follow his wife across to the car.

Angie sauntered back into the hotel and going upstairs to her bedroom looked up the telephone number of the Pendleton house. She came downstairs again to enquire if there was a public telephone in the hotel and was shown the small booth tucked away under the stairs. It contained a stool for the convenience of the patrons and sitting down, Angie switched on the light and got out the necessary coins.

The telephone only rang twice before the receiver was lifted and a light female voice answered. When Angie asked to speak to Pablo Pendleton there was a silence from the other end of the telephone and she was beginning to think they had been cut off when the voice asked politely but distantly, 'Is it important? I'm afraid he's rather busy at the moment.'

For a second Angie paused, a little shaken by the off-putting voice, then she pulled herself together and said firmly, 'I'm ringing about his interview with *Ladies' Graces*. It's all been laid on by my editor. We're expected, but I just wanted to confirm that it was all right to come over in the morning.'

'Hold on a minute,' and before she could explain further Angie heard the sound of the receiver being laid down. She waited two, three and then five minutes before a different voice, though again a feminine one, spoke into the receiver.

'I believe you wish to see my stepson.' This voice was softer and much more conciliatory in tone than the other. 'He can't come to the telephone at the moment, but he asks me to tell you that it's perfectly all right for you to come here to-morrow morning. But not before ten o'clock.'

Angie's thanks were a little perfunctory as she put her own receiver down and sat gazing at the instrument for two or three moments in silence. Then she grinned reluctantly as she got up and left the telephone booth. It was the first time she had been put quite so firmly in her place. She wasn't trying to see a busy man with regular appointments who would have to fit her in between callers. If she had understood Basil correctly, to all intents and purposes Pablo Pendleton was down here at his country house on holiday. Why the delay in seeing her, then? Unless of course he was a man who liked to lie late in bed. But this wasn't the impression that Angie had received from the information at her disposal and Robinetta, she remembered, had frequently complained about how early he liked to start work.

Angie shrugged her shoulders as she strolled over to the small reception desk to order early tea and a morning newspaper. Back in the lounge she ordered more coffee and sat down in front of the television set. She was not tired or ready for bed and while she didn't want to think of the coming interview she couldn't erase from her mind the questions which were crowding in. Perhaps a gripping television programme would take her mind off to-morrow.

But as she was drinking her coffee Angie suddenly recalled another pinpricking worry. In the turmoil of getting her off to Sardinia she had quite forgotten to tell Robinetta that Pablo Pendleton was on her list of interviews and her sister would undoubtedly think she had purposely left her in the dark. If Netta was still trying to contact her unco-operative boy-friend she certainly would not be pleased that Angie had been the one who managed to run him to earth. It might be a good idea to have a word with Mrs. Wilkinson, Angie thought, putting down her coffee cup, and returning to the little telephone booth, was soon speaking to the housekeeper, requesting her to forward letters but not to mention her whereabouts if Robinetta took it into her head to telephone from Sardinia.

As she went upstairs to her bedroom Angie wondered whether she had been wise. Would Robinetta think that she was being unusually secretive about this particular interview when she eventually discovered Pablo's whereabouts? It might be a good idea to-morrow evening to put a call in and see how Robinetta was getting along; ask Aunt Pam if her sister was feeling more cheerful, or still in the depths of despair about her latest entanglement. Angie had a horrible feeling Robinetta was not going to recover from this love affair with her customary bounce.

CHAPTER 2

ON the following morning Angie had just finished breakfast when Jack Bryant strolled into the hotel, and he raised his eyebrows when she told him they were not welcome up at the Pendleton house until ten o'clock. 'Since we've been told that we're not to put in an appearance until ten, let's turn up at five minutes past,' Angie grinned mischievously as she spoke.

'That gives us an hour to kill,' Jack said, 'so how about coming back to the caravan? No use in hanging about here, and it just so happens I'd have had to call back anyway. I've forgotten one of my cameras and I'll need it for the interior shots.'

Angie collected a coat, freshened her lipstick and checked the contents of her bag before joining him in the car. She normally carried a large shoulder bag in which she could fit a writing block and her tape recorder as well as personal necessities. 'I don't think this is going to be one of our nice smooth interviews,' she remarked as they sped along towards the farm where Jack's caravan was parked.

'What makes you think that?' Jack asked. 'You mean this business of not wanting us to turn up until ten? Perhaps he just likes to sleep late in the mornings.'

Before Angie could disillusion him Jack turned into the field and parked alongside his caravan. In two minutes the children were beside the car hugging and kissing Angie as she stepped out. 'Auntie Angie, we didn't think we'd be able to see you until this evening. Daddy said you'd be busy all day. Come into the caravan – Mummy's just washing up.'

Sylvia seemed as delighted at the unexpected arrival of Angie as her two children. 'We'll leave these to soak,' she said, drying her hands, 'and have another cup of coffee. I'm all for an hour's adult company if I've got to look after the children all day long on my own,' she remarked when Jack explained the stop off. 'There's plenty to do around here, but the undiluted company of the young sometimes palls,' and she grinned across at her husband who kissed her swiftly on the forehead before going to look out the camera he had left behind.

Angie sat down and looked round the van. She had been inside it many times before but always marvelled at the compactness of the interior fittings and the speed with which Sylvia could clear the family clutter and make the caravan look as neat as a new pin. It was a well-designed model with plenty of cupboards so that all necessary equipment could be stowed out of sight and it boasted, in addition, electric light and heating. An invaluable asset, Angie thought, for even in midsummer it could turn suddenly cold. Noticing her glance towards the heater Sylvia asked, 'Feeling chilly, Angie? Would you like me to switch it on?'

'No, I'm not cold. Just thinking how useful it was to have. I've slept in caravans which haven't any form of heating and sometimes been half frozen about three a.m.'

'I never knew you were a caravan expert,' Jack remarked as he joined the two girls, the missing camera in his hand.

'I'm not,' Angelina confessed, 'and to be honest it's not my idea of fun. But I have spent several holidays in caravans as a youngster. Mother and Dad were bitten by the bug once and we arranged one year to spend a month touring on the Continent. I'll never forget it. We broke down no less than eight times and the weather was terrible. As soon as we got back Dad sold the van, and that was the end of caravan holidays for the Snow family.'

At five to ten Angie put down her coffee cup and glanced at her watch. 'If you've everything you need we'd better make a start. Did you find out anything about the Pendleton family when you were asking the whereabouts of the house, Jack?'

'Very little,' Jack answered. 'They seem well respected in the village, but apart from that I could get little information. The house, as I told you, isn't far. Back up the hill and the first turning on the left. It's about half a mile further on on the right-hand side, or so your landlord says.'

'Let's go and find out if his directions are any good,' Angie said, getting to her feet, and she kissed both children, waved a hand at Sylvia and went outside to the car.

The directions turned out to be not quite so easy to follow as Jack had been told. True, they did have to go back through the village, and they did have to go up the hill and turn left, but it was some time before they discovered the Pendleton house. There were no names on the gateposts and in the end Angie got out and stopped a man who was cycling down the hill to ask for help. She returned to the car and Jack switched on the engine again to turn at her direction into the gateway some fifty yards ahead on the right. The driveway was heavily wooded on either side and they were almost up at the house before they could get a good look at it.

Pablo Pendleton's home turned out to be a square Georgian house built of the local stone with a big barn and several other outbuildings adjoining. It looked as if it might at one time have been a farmhouse, but there were no signs other than the outbuildings of farm activity and the gardens were neat and well kept. A circular drive wound up to the front door and getting out, Angie walked up the two steps and pulled on the old-fashioned bell-pull.

It was several minutes before the door opened and then a dark-haired middle-aged woman came out. She smiled as her eyes met Angie's and said, 'You must be the people from *Ladies' Graces* to see my stepson. There's no need to come into the house. If you just take the path round to the right here you'll come to the barn. Go straight in; he's expecting you,' and smiling once more she retreated into the house and closed the door again.

Angie turned round and met Jack's eyes. He had got out of the car holding his photographic equipment in his arms and his eyebrows were raised in a whimsical expression. Angie couldn't help it. She burst into a gurgle of mirth as she turned and started to walk towards the barn. Jack fell into step at her side.

'I think you're right,' he said in a low voice. 'This isn't going to follow our usual pattern.'

'Sssh!' Angie warned him. 'You never know who may be listening. Things look difficult enough as it is. Don't let's prejudice our chances, for goodness' sake!'

Three minutes' walk brought them to the barn. There was only one door visible, and when Angie knocked there was no reply. Jack reached above her head and gave a resounding bang on the door and immediately a voice shouted, 'Come on in!' Jack turned the handle and pushed Angie into the building so that she almost fell over the raised threshold. She stood for a minute just inside the barn trying to get her bearings.

It was much bigger than she had expected and most of the wall at the far end had been replaced by what appeared to be plate glass. By this enormous window two men were standing and both were watching the visitors in total silence. Angie was not as a rule overawed by circumstances, but the thought of the long walk down this floor towards these strangers made her hesitate for a second, and then she felt Jack's hand in the small of her back urging her forward and putting her chin in the air she walked towards the two men standing at the far end of the room.

They said nothing and neither smiled as she and Jack approached. One, the smaller and slighter of the two, was dressed in dark trousers and a navy blue pullover, the other man was wearing a lightweight brown suit with an apricot-coloured shirt and a brown and apricot tie. His hair was curly and considerably longer than that of the man by his side, but from their general resemblance to one another it was obvious that they were related.

Angie stopped about six feet away from them and stood in silence for a moment searching for words. Before she could make up her mind how to introduce herself the man dressed in pullover and trousers suddenly stepped forward and held out his hand. 'I'm Pablo Pendleton. I see you're punctual, at least.'

'Angelina Snow,' Angie said, stifling a tart retort to this opening sentence as she put her fingers into his.

Immediately the dark eyebrows over the sherry brown eyes were raised. 'Angelina Snow? I was under the impression that A. Snow was a man. The articles Basil Beavis showed me didn't strike me as having been written by a woman.'

'Is that meant as a compliment?' Angelina asked, as she handed her card over, at the same time raising her own eyebrows in deliberate imitation.

A slow smile started in the keen eyes staring down at her, but without answering her question Pablo Pendleton let go of her hand and turned away saying, 'But I haven't introduced my brother, Gordon. Gordon, this is Miss Snow from *Ladies' Graces*.'

Gordon Pendleton walked forward. He was not only taller and broader but handsomer than his brother. The sherry brown eyes, however, were identical and he smiled down at Angie, saying as if he really meant it, 'I'm very glad to meet you, Miss Snow.' There was no deliberate attempt to charm her, Angelina quickly realised, but nevertheless she lost no time in freeing her hand to turn and introduce Jack to both the men.

By this time the atmosphere had eased a little and

Angelina let out a silent sigh of relief just as Gordon Pendleton said, 'Well, it's been very nice meeting you and I shall probably see you again, but I must go now. I was on the point of leaving when you arrived. See you later, Pablo,' and he strolled off down the room, closing the door behind him with a mighty crash.

'Now that my brother's gone, we may as well get down to work at once. The sooner this business is over the better,' Pablo Pendleton announced autocratically as soon as the echo from the banging door had ceased, and Angie, angered by the barely tolerant tones, felt her temper rise. Seeing a chair against the window she deliberately went over and made herself comfortable and as she took out her writing materials heard Jack say, 'While you two are getting over the preliminaries I'll take some outside shots.'

'Only of the front of the house and the barn,' Pablo Pendleton ordered.

Jack had turned preparatory to going outside, but he stopped at these words and turned back to confront Pablo. 'But you look to have a beautiful garden at the back of the house. Some shots down there would be excellent.'

'As I said, film the front of the house only, if photographs you must have.' The tone of voice was rigidly polite, but there was no mistaking, Pablo Pendleton meant what he said, and Jack looked across at Angie enquiringly.

She glanced across the room, her mouth tight with ill-concealed exasperation, before saying quietly, 'Just do what you can for the moment, Jack. Perhaps Mr. Pendleton already has some photographs of the rear of the house he would be willing for us to reproduce.'

Jack shrugged slightly and went away, but as soon as the door had closed behind him Angelina spoke abruptly. 'I didn't want to ask in front of my photographer, but is there any particular reason why he shouldn't take some shots of the rear of your house?'

Pablo Pendleton did not answer for a moment or two. He

walked over to the big window beside her and looked out. When she thought he was not going to answer her question at all he turned his head and looked down. 'I wish I'd never agreed to give this interview at all. I can see all sorts of problems arising. But your editor was most persuasive and as he's done me a good many favours in the past I felt I could hardly refuse. However, there are one or two things we must get straight right from the start, Miss Snow. My family is not to be brought into this at all. Father is something of an invalid and has his rooms at the back of the house. I don't want him or his daily routine interrupted in any way whatever. If your photographer is permitted to roam around at will it could cause some inconvenience.'

Angelina looked back into the eyes watching her steadily. 'We have no intention of interfering with your family life in any way, Mr. Pendleton. In fact I personally was rather surprised we had to come down all this way to see you at all.' For the life of her Angie could not resist this crack. 'I'd understood the interview was to take place in London and I quite appreciate you wanting to keep your family out of the article, as naturally any side issue detracts from the central figure.'

There was a minute's pregnant silence before Pablo Pendleton answered. 'That was not my reason, as I think you realise.' His tone was quiet and deadly. 'I have some excellent photographs of the garden taken last summer,' he went on, 'and you're welcome to have your pick, but as I said before, I don't want your photographer wandering around at the back of the house. He can come and take as many shots inside here as he likes. That should keep him occupied,' and, as if that in his opinion was the end of the matter he walked over to his desk and sat down. He crossed his legs. 'Now then, where shall we begin?'

This wasn't going at all in the pattern of Angelina's usual interviews. To gain time she opened the folder on her knee and pretended to be studying the contents before she looked up to meet the hard brown eyes. 'Let's start with your childhood, shall we? It's usually as good a place as any to begin.'

She knew as soon as the words left her lips what construction would be put on her opening gambit and waited for the expected retaliation. Instead Pablo, who had been looking at the card on his desk, glanced up at her and began to smile mischievously. 'You think I'm behaving childishly? I apologise, Miss Snow, but though you may find it hard to believe I dislike people who are deliberately uninterested in the comfort of others,' and then he picked up the card which Angelina had given him on her arrival and read the name slowly. 'Angelina Snow. Now where have I heard that name before?'

Angelina waited. Should she tell him? But before she could make up her mind whether to admit that she was sister to his most famous model Pablo looked across at her. 'Snow! Of course. But you can't be Robinetta's sister.'

Accustomed though she was to surprise on people's faces when they discovered what a plain Jane Robinetta had for a sister, Angie felt a tiny prick of irritation as she did her best to smile back amiably. 'Yes, Robinetta is my sister, difficult though you may find it to believe,' she tried and failed to conceal the note of pique.

For a second there was silence and then Pablo Pendleton put the card down again and got to his feet. 'I'm sorry. Did that sound an unkind comparison? It wasn't meant to be, I assure you. We don't seem to be getting off on the right foot at all, do we? If I give you a full interview keeping nothing back co-operating in every way I can will you do something in return?'

'Such as what?' Angie was doubtful.

'Such as sitting to have your portrait painted.' He walked quickly across to her chair and before Angie could realise his intention had taken her chin in the palm of his hand and turned her face towards the light. 'Yes, good bones. Definitely good bones. I could make something of a portrait of you.'

Angie jerked her chin angrily away and wrote the date so forcefully on the pad balanced on her knee that the point of her pencil broke. 'I hardly think an exchange of bargains is necessary,' she snapped. 'You've already agreed with Mr. Beavis to do this interview. Why should I agree to sit for you in exchange for it?'

'All right, on your own head be it.' Pablo shrugged and turned back to his desk. 'You've already as good as accused me of being childish, so there'll be no picture and no interview. Or at least, not a satisfactory one,' his eyes gleamed, looking for a moment almost black.

'Blackmail?' Angie almost spat the word.

The hard eyes held a spark of ironic amusement. 'Oh, agreed. Certainly it's blackmail, but I intend to do a portrait of you.'

For several seconds Angie's angry eyes met his and she was chagrined to discover that hers were the first to fall. She could hold his glance for no longer than half a minute before she was forced to look away at the notes on her knee. As she scribbled a few words at random Pablo Pendleton walked back across the room until he stood beside her. 'Well, is it agreed?'

Angie looked up. 'Have I an alternative?'

He smiled grimly. 'Not really. Okay, let's begin. To-day we'll do your part and to-morrow early I'll expect you here for the first sitting.'

It was worse, much worse than even Angie had anticipated, difficult though she had known this job would be. She determined that as soon as an opportunity presented itself she would put a call through to London and tell Basil just what this impudent man had suggested, but she knew from that exchange of glances he would be as good as his word. If she refused to sit for a portrait he would without doubt be totally unco-operative, and all she would get out of him would be prosaic details without a single outstanding anecdote to amuse the readers.

Having gained his point Pablo became a different person, amenable and candid about his personal life. Angie soon had him talking easily about his childhood. He told her that his mother had been Spanish, that she had died when Gordon was a baby, that his father had married again two years later.

'I think I've met your stepmother,' Angelina interrupted, 'small and dark with a lovely smile.'

'Yes,' the mischievous look was back in Pablo Pendleton's eyes, 'my father liked his women small and dark. Mother was much the same,' and he glanced over his shoulder.

Angie followed the direction of his glance to see an imposing oil painting which she hadn't previously noticed hanging on the wall of the barn. It showed a young woman of obviously foreign origin, wearing a low-cut black evening gown. She had sparkling brown eyes and looked as if someone had just told her a joke which she found singularly amusing. It was an intriguing picture. The face wasn't strictly beautiful, but it caught and held one's attention, and Angie for a second found herself unable to look away.

'Yes, I believe she was fascinating,' Pablo said. 'I painted that from a photograph my father has. He says it doesn't do her justice.'

Angie glanced back at him to see that his eyes were on her face. 'Of course neither Gordon nor I really remember her. Bron's the only mother we've ever known.'

'Then school. You went away to boarding school, I believe.' Angie looked down again at her notes.

'Yes. Gordon and I were both sent at thirteen. When I left school it was to go straight on to art school, but my brother has brains and went on to university.'

'And your father. You said he's an invalid?'

There was a silence before Pablo answered, and once again his voice was harsh. 'I'd prefer you not to mention him in your article. He caught polio while he and Bron were on their honeymoon. He's been in a wheelchair ever since.'

'I'm sorry.' Angie felt she had trespassed.

'There's no need to be. It was a long time ago and he's resigned to his fate. In fact he's perhaps more mentally alert than the rest of us since the use of his legs was lost. It's just that he doesn't much like meeting strangers and he finds life from time to time very frustrating.'

'I can imagine.' Angie's voice was quiet.

'I hoped you might,' Pablo said. 'I'm relying on you to write this article without actually mentioning that Father is still living. It shouldn't be too difficult for you. I wouldn't have agreed to the interview if I hadn't been impressed by your professionalism.'

Angie looked up, genuinely surprised this time. 'Do you mean to say you've actually read some of the things I wrote in *Ladies' Graces*?'

'Of course. Otherwise I would never have agreed to give an interview in the first place. And I must say I'm still surprised that A. Snow is not a man. You put quite a masculine slant into some of the stuff I read.'

Angie looked down for a moment and she couldn't help a gleam of mischief coming into her eyes when at last she looked up. 'It must be something of a disappointment, then,' she said, 'to find that I'm only a woman. And if you read my articles you must have realised the importance our readers put on details of the interviewees' private lives? Some lead very humdrum existences and exciting celebrities are meat and drink to them.'

Pablo got to his feet and strolled over to the window. 'They'll be disappointed with me, then,' his tone was sardonic. 'I don't know where that photographer of yours has got to, but he must have had his fill of taking photographs of the front garden by now. What do you say we go and put him out of his misery?'

Angie glanced at her watch. She could hardly believe

it was already a quarter to one. 'You'll stay to lunch, of course,' Pablo invited as she got quickly to her feet.

'No, we can't impose.' She was sure he was only being courteous in extending the invitation.

'Nonsense! If you're going to be here all day you may as well stay to lunch. Bron will be delighted and have everything laid on, if I know her. Stuck out here she doesn't see many people, and in any case she's kept pretty busy dancing attendance on my father.'

Before Angie could interrupt he went on, 'You won't see him, however. He nearly always eats alone at lunch-time though he invariably joins us for dinner.'

They discovered Jack Bryant sitting on a garden bench enjoying the sunshine, apparently quite happy to be doing nothing for the moment. When Angie mentioned lunch he got to his feet and picking up his cameras followed them towards the front door. It was standing ajar and Pablo pushed it open so that Angie could walk into the house.

She glanced around for a second and then up at Pablo's face. 'Will we be permitted to take photographs in here?' she asked.

'Is it absolutely necessary?' The brown eyes looking down into hers held not a flicker of emotion. 'Instead of taking interiors of this house surely photographs of the barn and my studio in London would be more appropriate.' Angie knew she was being put in her place and deservedly so. It had been in the worst of taste to suggest that Jack should take photographs of the inside of the house, especially after Pablo Pendleton had taken the trouble to explain his reasons for not wishing his father's routine to be disturbed.

Before she could think up a remark to cover up her embarrassment Bron Pendleton came hurrying out of the door on the right hand side of the hall and she smiled with pleasure. 'Oh, you're staying to lunch. Good, I'm so glad. I thought Pablo might invite you as he knows how much

I enjoy visitors. Come along in. I'm sure you'd like a glass of sherry or a gin and tonic before we go into the dining room.'

The atmosphere was immediately lightened, and it was lightened still further when a very attractive young girl in her early twenties joined them and Bron Pendleton introduced her as, 'My husband's nurse, Christine Casement.'

'Secretary more like, don't you mean?' Pablo said as Christine accepted a glass of sherry from him. 'Dad doesn't need much in the way of nursing these days except a bit of help with his dressing. What's he been doing to you this morning, Christine? Keeping you hard at work as usual?'

Christine Casement threw back her long fair hair as she gazed up into Pablo Pendleton's eyes. She was tiny, a mere five feet, so was able to do it with ease, and Angie, looking across the room, wished she too was small enough to meet a man so much taller than herself that she would have to crane her neck as Christine was doing. All her male acquaintances, even James Stanscombe, were only of average height and she had yet to be dated by a man who towered above her. It must be an agreeable experience, she thought as she accepted the glass put into her hand. Make one feel small and helpless.

Lunch was a pleasant meal and as soon as it was over Jack went to take photographs of the barn while Pablo suggested to Angie that they went for a run in his car or took a stroll up through the woods behind the house.

'A walk, I think,' Angie decided as he pulled back her chair so she could get up. 'I don't usually eat until the evening,' she smiled down at Bron Pendleton, 'but your cheese soufflé was so delicious I'm afraid I've overindulged. A walk will be just the thing to stop me feeling sleepy.'

Fortunately she was wearing low-heeled shoes, so she followed Pablo up the steep track through the trees without fear for a sprained ankle. She was gasping for breath, however, when she reached the top and was glad when her companion suggested they sat a while on a convenient fallen tree and enjoyed a smoke.

When he held out his cigarette-case, however, Angie shook her head. 'I don't smoke, but I am glad to be able to sit down for a few minutes. I'd no idea the hill was so steep.'

'It's worth the view you get from here,' Pablo Pendleton remarked as he lit a cigarette and blew out a fine plume of smoke. 'Look down there.' Angie followed the direction of his pointing finger and for a few minutes obediently admired the view spread out before them, but her mind was on other matters and she suddenly turned and looked at him.

'I'd much sooner get on with my job and ask you a few questions. As a matter of fact I brought my tape recorder in case an opportunity like this turned up.'

'I was wondering why you decided to bring a ten-ton handbag on an afternoon stroll,' Pablo remarked dryly as she rummaged in the depths of her capacious bag and produced a small recorder, but Angie ignored his sarcasm and switching the knob to 'on' said, 'We've got to the point where you left art school. What made you turn to photography?'

Pablo grinned. 'To make money, what else? I'd always been interested in photography and Dad had kept me liberally supplied through the years with various makes of cameras as I became more proficient. But I actually went into it quite by accident standing in for a chap who went sick.'

'And the painting? I had no idea you painted.'

'Very badly, I fear, commercially speaking. In fact if I had to earn my living by it I'd probably starve to death. It's more in the nature of a hobby. I do it when I can get time off between assignments, like I'm doing at the moment.'

'But that picture of your mother looks so proficient.'

'You wouldn't say so if you were a competent art critic,' Pablo's smile held a hint of ridicule, 'which probably makes you wonder at my wanting to paint you,' he went on, quite ignoring the matter in hand and staring hard into her face. 'It's your skin tones. They're absolutely marvellous.'

Angie found that she was flushing. 'Never mind this portrait you want to do of me,' she said. 'If it's only a hobby it's not important. What is important are your usual daily activities.'

'Important to you maybe,' Pablo said serenely, 'not to me. I'm much more interested in getting you down on canvas. Who knows, it may turn out to be my chef d'oeuvre.'

'I think that's most unlikely,' Angie replied shortly. 'There must be far more suitable subjects for you to go to work on. What about Robinetta, for instance? You must have painted her.'

'As a matter of fact I haven't.'

Angie turned enquiring eyes on the man sitting beside her. 'Chocolate box beauty may be all very well for selling soap and cosmetics, but it's not my idea of what I want to get on canvas,' Pablo replied levelly. 'Now please don't take this as personal. Your sister has exceptional looks. It just happens they don't appeal to the artist in me.'

'But I thought....' Angie stopped and there was a moment's complete silence.

'Tell me? This is interesting.' Pablo's voice was intent.

'It doesn't matter.' Angie looked away, unwilling to meet his discerning gaze. 'It wasn't important. Now, getting back to how you took up photography?'

'Let's leave the next instalment until to-morrow.' His reply came after a pause during which Angie held her breath. 'I'm getting a bit bored with talking about myself.

Come on, I'll race you to the bottom,' and putting his foot on the stub of his cigarette he rose from their makeshift seat and set off with swift strides.

Hastily Angie thrust the tape recorder back into her bag and putting the strap over her shoulder ran after him. The tape recorder banged quite painfully across her hip as she hurried and she wished she had not troubled to carry it with her. There could be no more than three or four minutes' conversation on the reel and most of what had been said was unimportant and unlikely to add much information to her notes for the article. The only thing the tape would reveal was what Angie already knew. That this time she was dealing with an unco-operative as well as a complex subject quite unlike her previous interviewees.

Pablo took her back to the house by a roundabout way and it was almost four-thirty by the time they reached there. They found Jack sitting comfortably in the barn, his feet up on a chair, smoking and apparently quite happy, Angie thought angrily, to have been left to his own devices. When he saw them he got to his feet. 'Had a good walk?' he asked, and grinned as Angie grimaced.

'An energetic one at least,' Angie said shortly, and put her bag down on the corner of the desk.

'Well, if you don't mind,' Pablo's tones were perfectly polite, 'we'll call it a day. We can continue the interview in the morning. I expect you've got lots of notes you want to type up,' he added wickedly as Angie glanced suspiciously across the room at his face. 'Anyway, I'll see you here around a quarter to nine.'

'A quarter to what?' Jack looked surprised.

'Not you, Bryant. We shan't need you to-morrow. Just Miss Snow.'

Angie saw Jack's eyebrows beginning to rise and put in quickly, 'I'll explain later, Jack,' then turning to face Pablo, 'Very well, Mr. Pendleton. A quarter to nine,' and hoping she sounded unconcerned she added, 'Come along, Jack,

Time

we've been given a half holiday,' and walked out of the barn without a goodbye.

She did not speak again until they were safely out of earshot, then as Jack inserted the ignition key he turned and glanced fully at her. 'What was all that about?'

'Oh, let's go to your caravan and ask Sylvia to make us some tea,' sighed Angie, her temper beginning to cool a little. 'I shall only have to explain twice if I tell you now. You know she'll want to know why we're back so early. I'll tell you all about it then,' and no more questions from Jack would make her change her mind.

Rather to Angie's secret annoyance both Sylvia and Jack laughed heartily when she told them of the difficulties she was encountering in trying to get information out of Pablo Pendleton, and Sylvia was of course delighted at the prospect of having Jack to herself all the following day.

'I'll get the films developed that I've taken to-day when the kids are tucked up to-night,' Jack promised. 'I got some rather good ones in the barn when you and Pendleton were out of the way. I fixed up some lights and took a photograph of that picture on the wall as well. I imagine from the resemblance it must be either his mother or sister.'

'It's his mother, as a matter of fact, and he painted it from a photograph, or so he says.'

'Well, it's not bad, especially if he hasn't done it from life,' said Jack. 'I don't know if you've had a chance to examine it closely.'

'No, I haven't.' Angie remembered Pablo's disparaging remarks about his own work and was rather puzzled. 'I'll be interested to see what you've managed to get. Oh, and by the way, Jack, the reason he doesn't want us to take photographs of the back of the house is because his father's an invalid, although that snippet of information isn't for publication either. Apparently he caught polio some years ago and has been in a wheelchair ever since. However, our Mr. Pendleton says he has some photographs of the rear of the house and garden and he'll let us have them.'

'Seems as if I shall be having it easy on this job,' Jack remarked. 'Except for some interiors of his studio in London there isn't really much more I can do—unless he'd consent to pose with you, of course,' he grinned.

'I hardly think he's likely to agree to that,' Angie replied dryly, 'nor is he likely to pose on his own. The only chance we have of getting a photograph is by taking him unawares.'

'Even then it wouldn't do us much good,' Jack said. 'You know as well as I do that our particular clients have to vet all their photographs and we're only allowed to print the ones they say can go in. Even if I managed to catch our Mr. Pendleton off guard Basil wouldn't allow it to be slipped in. You know what a stickler he is.'

Angie nodded. She knew only too well that Basil Beavis stuck strictly to the book of rules, for naturally he had no wish to see the name of *Ladies' Graces* dragged through the law courts nor risk having a writ served on them. No, it had to be played straight. The only way in which she could get a photograph of Pablo Pendleton into the article would be to ask him straight out if he would allow Jack to take a photograph of him, and if he said 'No' that would have to be the end of the matter. Perhaps if she kept her part of their curious bargain, he would be prepared to stretch a point. She would have to see. Play it off the cuff and grab an opportunity if it came along.

Although Jack offered to come down early the following morning and run her up to the Pendleton house, Angie refused. 'No, it looks like being fine,' she said, glancing up at the sky as he dropped her off outside the inn. 'Make the most of the day with Sylvia and the kids. You know they'll enjoy having you to themselves for a whole day, Jack. I can either walk up to the Pendletons' or get the local taxi out if I'm running late. Don't worry.'

Jack waved goodbye and she walked inside, bathed and

changed before she enjoyed a solitary dinner and then went to bed early to write up her notes. Despite her optimism regarding the weather it rained heavily during the night, but when Angie finally stepped outside the following morning it looked as if the day might turn out fine after all. The road surfaces were drying rapidly and all around flowers and trees sparkled where rainwater still lay on their leaves.

Angie drew in a deep breath. How lovely everything smelled, she thought as she set off to walk up to the Pendleton house. She was nearly there when a van stopped beside her and a cheery voice asked 'Going far?' When she explained her destination the bakery van driver said, 'Get in. I'm going past the Pendletons', as it happens, and I can drop you off. Save you the rest of the walk up this steep hill, miss.'

Angie was only too glad to accept the lift and she slid into the seat beside the driver. He chatted cheerily about the weather and eyed her curiously as they turned into the lane leading to the Pendleton house. 'Not from around here, are you, miss?'

'No, just visiting,' Angie admitted. 'I'm staying down at the local inn at Llantarwyn. It's very comfortable there.'

'I'm not surprised,' the man nodded. 'I've known Jim Evans for years and his wife's one of the best cooks in the neighbourhood. You'll be well looked after there, I'm sure. Here we are,' and he drew up outside the gateway.

Angie thanked him as she got out, waved a brief goodbye as the van drove away and then turned to walk up the drive. As she reached the house she was considering whether to knock on the front door or go immediately to Pablo's studio when she heard him calling her name. He was standing in the doorway of the barn and he beckoned to her. Angie found it difficult to appear poised and unselfconscious as she went over to the doorway where he was critically watching her approach.

'Good morning! Punctual to the minute,' he said as he drew her inside the barn and closed the door. 'I can start my preliminary sketch while the light is at its best.'

It suddenly occurred to Angelina that she hadn't asked him what he wanted her to wear for the portrait, but she presumed that he had that well in hand as he seemed to have most things.

'If you just go behind that screen and undress,' he ordered her, 'you'll find a dressing-gown there. Put it on when you're ready, then I can arrange a pose against the draperies.'

Angie had been putting down her handbag and slipping out of the waterproof anorak she was wearing, but she turned at these words and gazed in sheer amazement. From Pablo's face she turned to stare towards the raised dais where a long length of brightly coloured material had been thrown in rather a haphazard fashion. Before she could find her voice Pablo continued, 'I thought I'd have you in a semi-recumbent posture, but with your face raised as if you're enjoying the sunshine. That way I can get the long line from chin to ear. As you haven't got long hair it won't have to be arranged to hang out of the way. I rather like the style. It's a change from to-day's usual fashion and you've got it so well cut it should be easy to paint in those swirls at the back.'

By this time Angie had found her voice. 'You're not really seriously expecting me to pose in the nude, are you? I assume that's your idea.'

Pablo turned round at her words, genuine surprise in his eyes. 'But of course—I thought you understood.'

'Well, I didn't, and as of now the bargain's off. I suppose that's the real reason you haven't painted Robinetta. Not because you consider her to be a chocolate box sort of beauty but because, like me, she would flatly refuse.'

'Did you really imagine I wanted you to sit fully dressed gracefully danging a rose or something equally hackneyed?'

Pablo asked sarcastically, and his brown eyes were hard and bright. 'Anyone can paint that sort of rubbish. I'm hoping one day to be able to afford to give up this photography lark, and turn a hobby into a lucrative business or at least become good enough to earn bread if not the butter. However, if all my models are as reluctant as you I shall get nowhere.'

Angie was shrugging herself angrily back into her anorak. She picked up her bag and turned towards the door. 'There must be hundreds—no, thousands of girls who would be perfectly willing to sit for you and pretend to enjoy the sunshine or whatever.' Her tones were as cutting as Pablo's had been. 'But I'm not one of them, thanks. So I take it this means the interview is over.'

'I didn't say so.' Pablo's tones were suddenly mild and Angelina eyed him suspiciously.

'I think the best thing I can do is phone Basil. The whole thing's quite ridiculous. So far I've learned nothing new about you. Yesterday's notes were quite useless. You hardly told me anything we didn't know already.'

She walked towards the barn door without waiting for a reply slamming it angrily behind her. She had worked up by this time such a rage that instead of turning and going straight down the driveway she inadvertently turned to the left, and when she came to her senses realised that she had trespassed into the forbidden rear garden of the Pendleton house.

She stopped in sheer amazement because it was quite unlike her expectations. Instead of a formal flat garden the ground sloped fairly steeply away from the house down towards a small stream lined with trees and flowers. A small wooden bridge spanned it and a garden seat had been placed in a shady spot where the path ended at the water's edge. Having come this far, Angie thought angrily as she took a face tissue out of the pocket of her anorak and dried the tears of anger from her eyes, she might as well go on. She didn't want to turn back and perhaps run into Pablo again so soon after speaking her mind. There must be some way via the bridge over the stream which would lead back to the village. However, when she got down to the bridge she found that the garden was securely fenced in on the other side of the stream. A six-foot brick boundary wall extended as far as she could see on either side and she knew that even with the risk of running into one of the Pendleton household she would have to retrace her steps back to the house and leave in a conventional manner via the front drive.

Before she did so, however, she decided to repair the ravages to her face, and walking down to the bench near the stream she sat down and took out her mirror and make-up. As she began to cover the traces of tear stains under her eyes she thought rather glumly about the phone call she would have to make to the London office. Basil would laugh when she told him how she had been cornered, but nonetheless he would be considerably put out. It was the first time she had failed to get a satisfactory interview from one of their V.I.P.s. The first time her tact had failed her. Blow Pablo Pendleton! He would have to turn out as difficult as Robinetta had confided, though not of course in the same way. There was little likelihood of him trying to tamper with her affections, Angie thought to herself. If it had been just that, she would have known how to deal with him.

She returned her make-up to her handbag and was getting to her feet when suddenly there came a startled shout above her and she rushed on to the path just in time to see a wheelchair roll from a verandah at the back of the house and begin to career down towards the stream. She saw Bron Pendleton dash out of the house followed by the nurse/secretary, Christine Casement, and the two of them run helplessly after the wheelchair which was now rapidly gathering speed. Its occupant appeared to be vainly trying to manipulate a lever on the right-hand side, but as far as

Angie could see from this distance, without success. The only way in which an accident could be prevented would be if she were to run from her vantage point below and manage to stop the runaway vehicle.

Angie dropped her handbag and ran up the path, but calculated that if she met the wheelchair head-on it would almost certainly knock her down but not necessarily stop. Turning at an angle, she began to run a little faster. The only sure way of stopping the runaway was to grab the side and hang on.

She was out of breath by this time and could hear her heart thumping with every step. There was a roaring in her ears as she reckoned she had exactly ten seconds to reach the wheelchair before it hurtled past. Making a last supreme effort, her hands caught and held the metal arm of the chair and Angie pulled with all her strength. The heavy chair skidded, teetered a moment and then fell heavily over on its side. Angie jumped backwards, but not quickly enough. She fell with the chair on top, felt a searing pain in her left leg, caught a glimpse of a bearded face and then blackness descended.

She recovered consciousness to the chatter of voices around her and the feel of damp grass under her cheek. Angie distinctly heard a male voice say, 'The ambulance will be here in a few minutes. Don't try to move her. Just cover her up,' and a moment later a rug was tucked around her. The pain in her leg was so intense that she kept her eyes closed. Somebody gently smoothed the hair back from her forehead and Bron Pendleton's easily recognisable voice said, 'You'll be all right soon, my dear. Just lie still.'

The next half hour was sheer torture, but eventually Angie found herself safely in the ambulance, and turning her head saw that a silver-haired man with a short pointed beard was lying in the opposite bunk. He smiled when he saw her eyes were open and said in a soft though very deep voice, 'This is an odd way to meet, my dear, but good morning, and thank you for saving my life. I'm Julius Pendleton, by the way.' Angie felt too exhausted to speak. She smiled faintly and closed her eyes again, concentrating on not crying out every time the ambulance hit a bump in the road. The journey seemed endless, but at last she was being wheeled into the hospital and it was not long before an anaesthetist was pushing his needle into her arm and once again Angie drifted into blessed oblivion.

When she came to she was lying in a small white-painted ward and her left leg was encased in plaster from thigh to toes. Complication upon complication, she thought as she gazed down at her leg and put a hand to her aching brow. What next? At least, she thought with wry amusement, it solved the difficulty of the abortive interview. Basil could hardly expect her to continue in her present condition and as soon as she was fit to travel she would have to get Jack to take her back to London.

She was soon to learn, however, that matters had been taken completely out of her hands. In the evening she received a visit from Bron Pendleton who came into the little room and drawing up a chair beside the bed, sat down and took Angie's hand between her own. There were tears in the soft brown eyes looking into Angie's as she said, 'My dear, words can't express our gratitude. You were an absolute heroine this morning. I don't know what would have happened if you hadn't been there at the precise moment that my husband's chair ran away. What were you doing down the garden, by the way?'

Angie smiled, 'Trespassing, I'm afraid. I turned down there quite by accident when I left the barn.'

'Well, it was a very fortunate accident for us,' said Bron. 'And now I've come to tell you that the surgeon says it will be at least six weeks before your leg is better, so I've arranged for you to come back with us to-morrow, when my husband will be well enough to return home.'

'Oh no!' Angie's startled voice interrupted her. 'I

couldn't possibly!'

Bron Pendleton smiled and spoke as if she were humouring an unreasonable child. 'You can't stay here, the bed is needed. Mrs. Evans at the Blue Boar is a good soul, but she hasn't time to look after someone sick. With Christine and myself on the spot what could be easier than to have you with us? I've already moved a bed into my little sewing room. It's just along the corridor from my husband's rooms and you can keep one another company.'

'But I'd intended going back to London.'

'And who would look after you there?' The Welsh accent was very pronounced as Bron's voice rose with indignation. 'I expect you either live alone or share with several other girls. If you're alone, who is to feed you while you're in this state, and if you share it will be like being ill in the middle of Piccadilly Circus because people will be coming and going all the time. And what about your interview with my stepson? I think it's as good a way as any of getting to know him so that you can write a really genuine first-hand article about his life and ideas. You'll see him in all his many moods if you're living under the same roof,' and Angie suddenly noticed that Bron's eyes were twinkling wickedly. 'That's settled, then.' The small woman rose to her feet. 'The ambulance is ordered for ten-thirty. Julius wasn't really hurt at all, only bruises and shock, but the doctor thought a night in hospital wouldn't hurt him,' and she said goodbye and left before Angie could think of any further excuses.

When she had gone Angie lay gazing out of the window for a moment or two until her thoughts were again interrupted, this time by the arrival of Jack Bryant. He came in, leaned on the end of the hospital bed and gazed silently at Angie for a moment or two. 'I must say this trip has been jinxed right from the start,' he said at last, and there was a wealth of laughter in his voice. 'First the man won't let us photograph the place, then he makes a bargain to paint you or he'll cancel the interview—and now you've saved his father from a broken neck and broken a leg yourself. I've had Basil on the phone and he tells me you're going to stay in the Pendleton house until you're better, or at least able to walk.'

'Basil said that?' Angie asked.

'What alternative have you unless I cart you back to London in the van, and I don't think that's a good idea,' Jack answered her, and he came over and sat down in the chair which Bron Pendleton had left beside the bed. 'We came down here to get an interview after all, didn't we? Let's take advantage of the fact that we've got an absolutely marvellous excuse to get right into the household. You'll get an insight into P. Pendleton, Esq. you'd never get in any other way.'

'But it seems mean to get the material like that,' Angie protested. 'I'd feel like a Paul Pry.'

'Why should you?' Jack interrupted her. 'After all, he hasn't treated you very fairly so far. I don't see why you should do the British thing and keep quiet about all his guilty secrets. If he has any, that is—I must say it will be interesting to see if there are any skeletons rattling away in the Pendleton cupboard. You'll be in a first-class position to winkle them all out.'

'How horrible you make it sound,' Angie said, and turned her head restlessly on the pillow. 'Go away, Jack, before I throw something heavy like a bedpan at you, and let me think.'

Jack got to his feet, laughing. 'I'll hang around for a day or two, but I don't think I'll be much more use here if you're going to stay with the Pendletons and I may as well go back to London.'

'Oh, don't desert me!' Angie tried to sit up and then winced at the pain in her leg. 'Wait for a couple of days at least, Jack.'

'All right,' Jack promised as he went towards the door.

'See you to-morrow some time, black grapes and all,' and he grinned as he closed the ward door behind him.

The following day Julius Pendleton and Angie were taken home by ambulance. She was carried along the downstairs corridor and put to bed in a comfortable little room overlooking the garden which had obviously been hastily converted into a bedroom. Angie discovered that her suitcase had been brought up from the inn, and when she asked about the bill Bron Pendleton waved aside her anxious questions.

'We'll talk about all that later,' Bron was patently putting off the discussion. 'The doctor says you must be kept quiet for a day or two. Now I'm doing to see to my husband. He's still annoyed with himself for letting his chair get too near the edge of the verandah when the brake was off and causing the accident. I'm going to draw the curtains for a while. Try and have a doze before lunch. I'll bring you a tray about one. Anything you particularly fancy?'

Angie shook her head, quite at a loss for words. It was obvious that Bron was thoroughly enjoying the situation of having two invalids to look after, both quite unable to disobey her commands, and Angie wondered what her hostess would have thought had she told her of the comfortable home she shared with Robinetta and that had she gone back to London Mrs. Wilkinson would have nursed her admirably. Why had she given in so easily to Bron's suggestion? It wasn't simply the matter of the magazine article which had kept her silent nor, she admitted honestly to herself, the thought of Basil's displeasure if she failed on the job. Despite her better judgement, Pablo Pendleton's character intrigued her, and the accident gave her a perfect excuse to study him at closer quarters.

For the next four days Angie was looked after very competently by Bron Pendleton and Christine Casement. She saw nothing of the Pendleton brothers, although she heard heavy male footsteps passing her door from time to time, but on the fourth morning after the accident when her leg was feeling much more comfortable, there was a knock on her door about noon and Pablo and Gordon Pendleton came into the room together.

'How's the heroine of the piece this morning?' Gordon asked, and his eyes twinkled as he came towards the bed. Leaning on the bed end, he smiled down at Angelina. 'Mother thinks you're well enough for some company this morning, so we've orders to carry you along so you can sit and talk to Dad for a while. Feel up to it?'

'I feel perfectly well,' Angie said firmly. 'My dressing-gown's over there. Would you give it to me, please?'

Though she had spoken in Gordon's direction it was Pablo who picked up the dressing-gown hanging over the back of a chair and walking over to the bed helped Angie to put it on. As he leaned down her eyes met his and she flushed painfully, suddenly remembering their last encounter. But Pablo smiled back quite guilelessly as if unaware of any embarrassment, and as soon as she was buttoned into the long concealing garment both men helped her swing her legs gently over the side of the bed and Gordon picked her up in his arms. Pablo contented himself with opening the door and protecting the plaster cast as they left the room.

They must have looked so ludicrously funny as they manoeuvred her along the corridor that Angie's sense of humour suddenly bobbed to the surface and she began to giggle helplessly.

'Don't wobble, for goodness' sake,' Gordon warned her, 'otherwise I'm liable to drop you. It's not going to be easy in any case getting you into Dad's sitting room.'

With an effort Angie controlled her mirth and the three of them went slowly down the corridor and into a big airy room at the back of the house where Julius Pendleton was sitting in his wheelchair looking expectantly towards the door. Another smaller folding wheelchair had been put beside his own and Gordon lowered Angie gently into it. When she was comfortably settled with a light rug covering her legs and feet, Pablo stood back, saying as he did so, 'There you are, Dad. She's all yours,' and taking his brother by the arm they left Angie facing her host.

She sat and studied him in silence for several moments, refreshing her memory. She had only the briefest recollection of his face from their earlier meetings and had been too concerned with showing no sign of the pain caused by the jolting of the ambulance to pay him much attention. Now she was able to stare for as long as good manners permitted, and she found she liked what she saw.

The man with the silver hair and neatly trimmed grey beard sitting in the invalid chair must have been a tall, powerful man before poliomyelitis struck him down, and Angie smiled as she suddenly noticed Julius Pendleton was looking her over with reciprocal interest. Apart from a large bruise on his right cheek, already turning yellow, he showed no outward signs of the accident, and Angelina was surprised out of her thoughts by his low chuckle into realising she had been silent a little longer than was strictly good manners.

'In two minds about whether I was worth saving?' he asked, and smiled as Angie's eyes widened at his words. 'Don't look so surprised—I'm only teasing. I'm eternally grateful for what you did, and sorry it landed you with this,' he indicated Angie's leg.

'It was my own fault, you know,' Angie said, 'but I couldn't think of any way to stop the chair except catching it sideways. It never occurred to me at the time that it might hurt you too. I'm sorry about your bruised face.'

'Oh, that's nothing. I fully expected as I careered down the path to end up in the morgue. And quite honestly, my dear, I don't see any other way you could have stopped the chair except in the way you did. I'm a good weight, you know, and my old chair was pretty heavy. What do you think of this new one the lads have got me? It's the very latest,' and he looked down with pride at the contraption of steel and chromium in which he was sitting. Angie recognised it as one which she had seen recently on television. 'Much more streamlined, wouldn't you say, and it's got a very reliable brake too. Of course it was my own fault for going too near the edge of the verandah. My wife has warned me on several occasions and told me I was tempting providence. Man-like I took no notice,' and he grinned very boyishly across at Angelina. 'I must say it was lucky for me you decided to explore the garden on that particular morning.'

Angie looked down at her hands for a second and then glancing up stared straight into his bright blue eyes.

'I wasn't really exploring your garden,' she admitted, 'I was trespassing. Your son had told me quite categorically that he didn't want you to be disturbed and that neither I nor my photographer were to go into your private garden. I was thinking of something else and walked down there quite by accident.'

'Well, a very fortunate accident it turned out to be for me.'

'That's what your wife said.' Angie smiled faintly as she recalled her conversation with Bron. She was just about to add her thanks for their kindness in insisting that she returned here on being discharged from the hospital when a voice from immediately behind her said softly, 'You two have had ample time in which to apologise to each other and exchange compliments, so I'm sure you're both now in need of a spot of fortification. Sherry, Miss Snow?'

Angie turned her head sharply. Until he spoke she had been entirely unaware that Pablo Pendleton had come back into the room. He was standing beside her now, a glass in one hand and a bottle in the other. 'Medium dry suit you?' he asked her as their gaze met.

Angie nodded speechlessly as the glass was filled and

put into her hand. By the time Pablo had filled two more glasses Bron Pendleton had come hurriedly into the room. 'Good, I see they've given you a drink,' she said. 'We'll have lunch in here. I'll bring it in on the trolley and we can eat it picnic fashion on our knees. You don't mind, do you?' she looked across at Angelina.

'Anything suits me,' Angie replied promptly. 'I don't eat much lunch as a rule.'

'Well, we always have something moderately filling, but I won't give you too large a helping,' Bron Pendleton promised as she hurried away again.

Almost immediately to Angie's relief Gordon Pendleton came back into the room. She was still not at her ease with Pablo and would have really liked a longer conversation with his father to get to know him better. She sat quietly listening to the three men talking companionably together until the door opened once again and Bron Pendleton and Christine Casement came in pushing a large trolley between them.

On it were a variety of cold meat and salads, and on the bottom shelf an open fruit tart and a jug of cream with a covered pot of coffee beside it. A small table was set up beside Angie's chair and a plate of food put in front of her, all cut up for easy handling, Angie noticed. She smiled inwardly to herself. Bron Pendleton must be so used to serving up meals for a semi-invalid that she had automatically done the same for Angie herself. Refusing mayonnaise or chutney, Angie picked up a fork and began to eat.

The atmosphere during the meal was more relaxed than she had anticipated. The two Pendleton sons were very much at ease with their father and gently teased him about his clumsiness in allowing his wheelchair to run away and injure a perfectly innocent bystander, and finished by asking him whether he thought himself capable of handling the new one.

'Any fool could use this one,' Julius Pendleton said, and he began to demonstrate his boast by manoeuvring it dexterously around the room until at last his wife protested, 'Oh, for goodness' sake, Julius! Stop behaving like a schoolboy. Finish your lunch. Whatever will Miss Snow be thinking about with you behaving like a six-year-old?'

'If she's got any brains at all, as I'm sure she has,' Julius Pendleton replied promptly, 'she'll be thinking that you're a regular nig-nag, my dear, and wondering how on earth I put up with you.'

Angie smiled. Nothing less like a henpecked husband than Julius Pendleton could possibly be imagined. Despite his crippled state he was obviously master in his own household, and it certainly was not his wife who wore the trousers. As soon as lunch was over and the trolley had been wheeled out Bron insisted that Christine took Angie back to her own room so she could have a short nap. She was feeling very wide awake, but she acquiesced and allowed Julius Pendleton's nurse to push her back along the corridor in the wheelchair and help her get back on the bed.

'Think you'll be all right now?' Christine asked as she drew the curtains across the window and tucked the eiderdown carefully over Angie's legs. Sensing that she was eager to be on her way, Angie nodded and murmuring, 'Thank you very much for helping me,' she watched as Christine quickly went out of the room again.

In spite of the fact that she did not feel sleepy Angie closed her eyes and went over the conversations which she had overheard that lunchtime. They seemed a happy family and Julius Pendleton, despite his infirmity, did not appear at all to be the remote recluse she had imagined from Pablo's insistence that he was not to be disturbed in any way. Indeed she could hardly understand why she had been prevented from meeting her host before the accident. He looked the sort of man who would not only welcome visitors, but indeed be interested in anybody new to the district. Had there been some other reason why Pablo had not wished her to meet his father? If so, at the moment it totally escaped her and she dismissed the matter from her mind, deciding that since she was lying comfortably and had nothing else to do it might not be a bad idea to accept Bron's suggestion to have a few minutes' sleep.

The effort of being sociable for the first time for days must have taken more toll of her than she realised, because it was over an hour later before she opened her eyes again, glanced at the clock and saw she had slept far longer than those 'two minutes.' Someone was tapping gently on her door and when she raised her head and called 'Come in' Pablo Pendleton's head appeared. Seeing that she was awake, he walked quietly into the room and stood leaning against the wall opposite the bed, looking across at her in complete silence.

Intimidated by his unswerving stare, Angie struggled to sit up, but found that she had the greatest difficulty in doing so with an immobilised leg. Instantly, seeing her predicament, Pablo unhooked himself from the wall and was beside her in two swift strides. He put his hands around her waist and very gently but steadily raised her until she was in an upright position, then holding her steady with one hand, plumped the pillows into the small of her back and let her relax against them.

When he was sure she was comfortable he stood back. Although his face was immobile there was a smile in his eyes and Angie, glancing fleetingly at him, thought how kind he looked and wished that she could believe it to be a real indication of his character. It was more likely, she thought as she fussed with the bedclothes in order to give her hands something to do, that he was looking at her with that particular gleam in his eyes for some ulterior motive as yet unspoken, and she was determined not to be the first to start the conversation. She did not have very long to wait. Pablo hooked a chair out from against the wall, put it beside the bed and sat down astride it, leaning his folded arms along the back and looking at Angie with the smile still very evident in his brown eyes. She was sure his kindly expression was merely to disarm as soon as he spoke.

'Have you forgiven me yet, or was it just a sudden attack of mock-modesty?' and then as she opened her mouth to speak said, 'Spare me the "what do you mean" routine. You're much too intelligent a girl to use that tack.'

Angie looked up and her eyes were bright with anger. 'I'm no humbug, if that's what you're trying to imply,' she said, 'nor am I given to attacks of mock-modesty. I just don't take my clothes off at the drop of a hat, even if it's going to be for the sake of art.'

To her surprise, Pablo gave a low chuckle, and getting to his feet said, 'This discussion could turn out to be very interesting and we must continue it at a more convenient moment. However, I only came to see if you were awake because your tame photographer wants a few words with you. I think he intends returning to London in the morning. Feel up to seeing him?' and he turned to the door.

'Of course,' Angie replied promptly. 'Let him come in at once, please,' glad of her escape and not knowing how peremptory was her tone of voice until Pablo gave a mock imitation of a butler's bow of acknowledgement and backed out of the doorway.

She had schooled her expression by the time the door opened again and Jack Bryant came in. Her eyes looked beyond him, but Pablo, much to her relief, had not returned with her visitor.

'I'd have come to see you before now, old girl,' Jack explained as he advanced towards the bed and turning the chair which Pablo had used sat down facing her.

'Every time I called Mrs. Pendleton insisted that you'd had a bad shock and it would be better for me to wait. I must say Pendleton himself has quite made up for his previous lack of co-operation. He's given me a whole sheaf of marvellous pictures of the garden and rear views of the house, he even deigned to pose outside the door of the barn, and I'm to have as much time in his studio in London as I wish, to take some interior shots. I spoke to Basil on the phone yesterday and he agrees that I can serve no useful purpose in staying down here. Has he been in touch with you?'

'Not yet,' Angie admitted, 'but it's quite possible that he's phoned and Mrs. Pendleton hasn't told me. As you can see,' and she glanced round the small room, 'they've fixed this room up as a temporary bedroom and it doesn't boast an extension. When I'm more used to getting myself about, either in that thing over there,' and she waved her hand towards the wheelchair which Christine had left in a corner of the room, 'or on crutches, I'll perhaps be able to get to a phone. How's Sylvia, by the way?'

'Fighting fit,' Jack assured her, 'and the kids too. In fact it's been a jolly good break for them and Sylvia came up here for a meal with me last night. Mrs. Pendleton arranged for someone to sit in at the caravan with the children.'

Angie's eyes widened. The Pendletons *were* being noble all of a sudden, more than making up for the lack of enthusiasm with which she and Jack had first been greeted. Surely it could not all be on account of the fact that she had saved Julius Pendleton from a nasty crack? It was useless to cogitate on the reasons for the Pendletons' present behaviour, and in any case Angie had more important matters on her mind.

'I suppose you wouldn't give Wilkie a ring when you get back to London?' she asked Jack. 'She'll be wondering what on earth's happened to me. I haven't been able to telephone and I didn't feel like writing.'

'Of course I'll ring her up,' said Jack. 'Better still, if you like to scribble her a note I'll take it round and give her news of you first hand.'

'Oh, that is good of you.' Angie sank back relieved. 'I need some things if I've got to stay here tied by the leg,' and she smiled wryly down in the direction of her plaster cast. 'Give me a ball-point and a piece of notepaper and I'll scribble her a few lines.'

Jack obligingly fetched writing materials and waited patiently as Angie wrote a note to her housekeeper explaining the reason for her continued absence and the new address to which mail was to be forwarded. 'Incidentally, Jack, you might warn her that if Robinetta should ring from Sardinia not to mention my whereabouts but tell her I'll ring back.'

'Will do,' promised Jack, getting to his feet and taking the outstretched envelope. 'Sylvia was going to come in and say goodbye to you herself, but it would have meant bringing the kids too and I thought they might be a bit much for you. She asked me to give you her love.'

Angie smiled, 'Thanks. Tell her I'll see her as soon as I get back to London. I don't intend staying longer than it takes to get the article finished, even if I have to crawl back to London on my hands and knees.'

Jack grinned as he reached the door. 'You've only to say the word, old girl, and I'll pop down and collect you. Don't worry. We won't leave you at the mercy of the enemy for ever, but get the story if you can. We may as well wrap it up as we've come this far.'

Angie nodded as the door closed behind him. She sat for five or ten minutes staring straight in front of her, and then, suddenly making up her mind, she glanced around to see that the crutches which had been supplied by the hospital were well within her reach and she felt sure she could manage to stand up against the side of the bed if she were careful. Her dressing-gown was at her feet and leaning over she drew it slowly towards her. It took several minutes to get into the dressing-gown, but at last it was accomplished and Angie threw back the bedclothes. Slowly and laboriously she got her left leg over the side of the bed and then sat with both feet on the floor, staring ruefully at the clumsy-looking plaster cast. Placing her hands on the bed, she pulled herself upright and stood with the uninjured leg braced against the mattress. By stretching out an arm she was just able to reach the first crutch with her finger tips and drawing it slowly towards her she managed to prop it under her right arm. It was easy then to turn and get hold of the other crutch and tuck it under her other arm.

Once she had the crutches firmly in place Angie, a determined expression in her eyes, started off in a perambulation of the room, at first cautiously but gradually with more and more confidence. She had done three circuits of the bed and had walked over to lean against the window sill for a brief rest when the door opened and Pablo Pendleton appeared carrying a small tea-tray.

For a second surprise showed on his face as he saw Angie standing at the window and then a slow grin replaced the astonishment in his eyes as he pushed the door to behind him with one foot before walking over to deposit the tea-tray on the dressing-table. 'Getting fed up with being incarcerated, are you?' he asked. 'I don't blame you. It must be the very devil to be stuck here literally tied by the leg. You've decided to try your wings to-day,' he commented, and gesticulated towards the crutches under Angie's arm. 'And you're looking a lot better for it, if I may say so.'

Angie, her face flushed by exertion and surprised that Pablo had echoed her very words, gave a spontaneous laugh. 'Thanks! I feel fine to-day. Your stepmother has kept me in cotton-wool since I got back from the hospital, but I want to try and fend for myself a bit and not spend all my time being wheeled around in that,' and she pointed with one finger to where the wheelchair stood. 'I shall have to get used to having this wretched thing on my leg for a week or two, so I thought I might as well practise with my crutches while I was alone.'

'Thought you'd be free from interruption, I take it?' he asked mockingly. 'Well, at this rate you'll be galloping all over the place in no time.'

'I hope you're right. I must say they're easier to manage than I'd thought,' Angie replied, and pushed herself away from the window frame in an over-confident attempt to get back to the bed. It was her undoing. One crutch slipped away from under an arm, she stumbled and suddenly found strong arms supporting her.

She looked up to discover Pablo's face within inches of her own. 'I said you'd soon be galloping around like a two-year-old, but there's no point in falling flat on your face right now to prove me right,' he commented, then stopped suddenly as Angie didn't speak but stayed gazing up at him quite silently. 'You know, my dear, I will paint you while you're here, clothed or unclothed—I don't care which. You really have got the most amazing bone structure and the most beautiful curve to your lips I've seen on a girl for a long time,' and before Angie could realise his intention Pablo bent and pressed a firm kiss directly on her mouth.

Instantly she leaned as far back as she was able and the words seemed to jump involuntarily from her mouth. 'How despicable to take advantage of me like this—and what makes you think I'm willing to exchange kisses with you? Isn't one sister enough, or do you have to have both scalps dangling from your belt?'

For a moment there was absolute silence and Angie suddenly realised the supporting hold had become a grip and that iron fingers were biting into her. After a long, almost insupportable silence Pablo's grip slowly relaxed and she was steadied against the bed as he bent, still in complete silence, and retrieved the crutch which she had dropped. As he reinserted it under her arm, Angie looked up to see that his eyes, usually kindly in expression, were as cold and hard as two brown pebbles.

'I'm at a complete loss to understand what that extraordinary remark of yours can mean,' he said as he went over to the dressing-table and began to pour out a cup of tea. 'I can only conclude that Robinetta has been telling you some exaggerated and probably quite ficticious story. Come on, you'd better get back to bed. You're obviously not as fit as you imagine.'

Angie sat down on the bed, suddenly unsure of herself and more than a little taken aback by the fury in his voice. Pablo turned back the bedclothes and as soon as Angie had straightened the pillows removed the crutches, helped her injured leg on to the bed and then drew the bedclothes swiftly back into position before he handed her the cup of tea. 'I suggest you sip this slowly. Perhaps it will soothe your obviously overwrought nerves. I never thought to hear such a brouhaha over a simple kiss. I should have thought someone of your intelligence would have learnt by now to take a compliment gracefully.'

Angie put the cup and saucer down on the bedside table, for her hands were shaking uncontrollably and by this time she was almost as angry as Pablo. 'If I thought you meant it as a compliment...' she began, when Pablo held up his hand.

'I'm not prepared to continue this conversation. To start with, I'm told you're to be treated gently as you've had a shock and Bron will have my life if she thinks I'd done anything to upset you. Since it's obvious my presence annoys you, I'll remove it forthwith,' and he strode out of the room, shutting the door quietly behind him.

This in itself only annoyed Angie further, for she had

fully expected him to slam the door as he left, and it was quite three minutes before she felt calm enough to turn and pick up the cup of tea and hold it to her quivering lips. She might have been drinking red ink for all the pleasure it gave her. Why had she been so foolish and blurted out such a revealing remark? Her whole idea had been to keep quiet about the fact that she knew there had been anything between Pablo and her sister. Now he would be well aware of the real reason behind her animosity and she would learn nothing and get nowhere with him. He might even write her off as jealously feminine and put an end to the whole project.

But the next morning she discovered that nothing was further from Pablo's mind. As soon as she had breakfasted Angie was helped into her clothes by Christine Casement, lifted on to the wheelchair and pushed out to the barn. There she found Bron busy dusting and vacuuming under Pablo's obviously tolerant supervision. 'Don't mind me, you get on with what you're doing,' and Pablo's stepmother went on tidying some, if not all, of the paraphernalia which littered the large studio.

At least, Angie thought as she got out paper and pen, Pablo was not the sort of man to refuse to have anything touched or to mind an occasional cleaning up operation. On the contrary, Angie noticed he was watching with indulgence in his eyes as his stepmother stacked canvases in a more convenient and out-of-the-way position and liberally used furniture polish on those surfaces she had managed to free of the clutter of paints, brushes, canvases and papers.

His eyes were alight with laughter as he turned to Angie and said in a low voice, 'This ought to make an interesting paragraph in the article—"photographer's stepmother takes over studio—polishes off his best work!"' Since Bron was at that precise moment heaping dozens of blown-up prints into piles one on top of another, Angie couldn't help a chuckle escaping, although she had been determined to keep future encounters with Pablo on formal and very businesslike lines. It was impossible, she was discovering, to nurture resentment or to keep this man at a distance if he wished otherwise. Apparently yesterday's unhappy episode was to be quite forgotten, completely wiped off the slate as if it had never been.

In the next few days Angie's life assumed a regular pattern. Every morning, as soon as she had dressed and eaten a light breakfast, she was wheeled down to the barn. Bron would usually be present for the first hour or so, but after morning coffee, Angie and Pablo would be left on their own until lunchtime. Only one thing differed from previous interviews. Now while Angie asked her questions and Pablo discussed details about his life and work, he sketched on a large pad balanced on his knee. Though Angie knew herself to be the subject of the many large sheets of cartridge paper which he covered, Pablo neither asked her permission nor commented about what he was doing. When at last she did venture a half quizzing remark to the effect that she hoped he wasn't drawing the plaster cast, Pablo neither answered nor indeed gave any sign that he had even heard, waiting patiently for her next question about his professional work, so that Angie was forced to revert to the business in hand.

Information she required he now gave simply and straightforwardly with no return to the intimacy which had crept briefly into their relationship after Angie had slipped in her bedroom two or three days earlier. Nor had he referred again to Robinetta, either directly or indirectly, and this gave Angelina food for thought. She had received a thick packet from London containing mail readdressed by Mrs. Wilkinson, but it had not included word from her sister. Robinetta was not much of a letter writer at the best of times and Angie, anxiously scanning the envelopes for Robinetta's familiar scrawl, was relieved to see that at least there was a long screed from Aunt Pam.

'You'll be glad to know,' she wrote, 'that Netta appears to be recovering slowly. She's not quite her usual bright and breezy self, but as good luck would have it, some Italian friends of Luigi have come to spend a month on the island and they've got two very attractive sons in their mid-twenties. The family came up to dinner the night after Netta arrived and both the boys took one look and are now vying for her favours, so she's not being given much time to mope. If Guido and Marino are not up here first thing in the morning to coax Netta down to the beach for a swim, they're driving her all over the island. All in all they're giving her very little time to dwell on her own affairs.'

Angie put the letter down and gazed out of the window rather thoughtfully. She was glad her sister had something to take her mind off the unhappy love affair, but it didn't necessarily mean that she was consoled. Netta had a peculiar habit of digging her heels in, particularly if a boy-friend looked like breaking things off, and could be really dog-in-a-manger. Somehow or other she must get Pablo talking about Robinetta. So far he had hardly mentioned the various models he used and then only in a general sort of way, without naming any particular girl. Angie didn't know whether it had been done on purpose or whether she was just imagining that he had kept off the subject of personalities deliberately.

Every evening she retired to her room fairly early and typed up her notes. Gradually a draft of her article was taking form and beginning to have some shape and depth. But whether with a prejudice against Pablo already formed she had really got a glimpse of his true character Angie could not decide, and whether Basil would be pleased with her work she had no idea. She wished desperately that she could hand the whole interview over to somebody else, but she knew at this stage it would be an impossibility. And in any case, what possible reason could she give Basil for doing so, since she was installed actually in the house and the Pendleton family were being good enough to nurse her? She had no real excuse for suddenly returning to London with her work only half finished and to add to the complications she had an appointment at the local hospital in a couple of days to see if the leg was knitting properly and she would have to stay for that at least.

The following morning while Angie scanned her notes and clarified one or two matters Pablo Pendleton was busy at the table cleaning a pile of dirty paintbrushes. Glancing across and finding him absorbed, Angie watched his bent head, wondering as she did so what there was about him to attract her volatile and beautiful sister.

You couldn't describe Pablo Pendleton as handsome; his appearance was not outstanding and his hair, though well cut, was by no means trendy or in the latest and most fashionable style. Robinetta as a rule liked her escorts to be in the forefront of fashion, if not ahead of it, and often ridiculed anyone she considered out of touch. Nor could it be the kindness which Angie had noted in Pablo's eyes which would appeal to Robinetta's capricious heart, for she usually looked only for admiration in the eyes of her men friends. And it wasn't because he could pose for Mr. Universe either, Angie thought, for Pablo was only of average height and while he boasted broad shoulders and slender hips, he was wiry rather than muscular in build.

But that there was something about him even Angie could feel, prejudiced though she was; something about the man's whole personality which attracted one against one's will. Animal magnetism, she supposed, her lips twisting in a smile at her own thoughts as she glanced down at her notes, discovering to her own annoyance that she was wrenching her eyes away from the silently working figure with some difficulty. This would never do, she warned herself, and looked up again to continue her interrogation.

Pablo answered her last question rather abstractedly as

he wiped a brush on an old rag and then looked up to meet her eyes. 'What was all that thoughtful silence about a few minutes ago?' he asked, and Angie looked away at once. Not for all the world would she let him guess that she had been dwelling on his appearance and cogitating on the possible hidden facets of his character which might be likely to attract a girl as temperamental as her sister.

A few days later Pablo chauffeured Angie to the hospital. It wasn't necessary for Julius Pendleton to have a check-up since he had sustained no serious injury and by now his bruised face had completely healed. To Angie's secret astonishment she wasn't kept waiting at the hospital more than a few minutes before she was ushered in to see the specialist. He had the plaster removed, examined her leg carefully and then further X-rays were taken before a fresh plaster cast was applied to the injured limb. It was all over in a remarkably short space of time and not even in the overworked X-ray department was Angie delayed for long.

She remarked on the efficiency at the hospital as Pablo headed the car in the direction of Llantarwyn, and turned surprised eyes on him as he chuckled. He must have felt her questioning glance because his eyes left the road briefly and met her own.

'You'll find as you get to know him better that Father has a way of getting things done, disabled though he is. You didn't imagine he would sit idly by knowing you might wait in a queue perhaps for hours, did you? Your visit was all laid on days ago.'

'You mean I got preferential treatment and that some of those other patients had to wait because of me?' Angie's voice rose with indignation.

'Not at all.' Angie had to wait in simmering silence as Pablo, his whole attention taken by a traffic snarl-up, paused in his explanation. Then as the car in front began to move, he went on, 'My father has known Alex Richards, the orthopaedic man you saw, for years, so it was only natural that he should arrange for you to be seen at a time convenient to us all. Don't get uptight. You inconvenienced nobody by being dealt with so promptly and no one missed their turn because of you. Something of a radical, though, aren't you, Miss Snow?'

'Not at all,' Angie drew a deep breath and made a conscious effort to keep her temper. 'I'd hate to be pushed aside myself to make way for some latecomer no more entitled to privileged treatment than myself, so I wouldn't dream of consciously doing it to others.'

She was not aware that she had emphasised the word 'consciously' until Pablo glanced at her flushed face and grinned again. Her flush deepened. He was laughing at her and his amusement was heightened by the fact that he knew she found the situation unpalatable since to-day's hospital arrangements had been made solely with her welfare at heart and good manners made it impossible for her to complain to Julius Pendleton for his forethought. How much she wished she had never been persuaded to accept the Pendleton hospitality and even more that it had not been necessary for her to do so. It would have to be a leg broken in the accident. A collarbone, an arm, even several ribs and she could have stayed at the village inn to do her job as she had originally planned. Angie turned away to hide her face from Pablo's keen eyes, more determined than ever to finish the article as quickly as possible and get Jack Bryant to come and take her back to London. In the peace of her own flat she could resume her usual daily routine and try and forget the impossible Pendleton family.

As soon as lunch was over Angelina excused herself and went to her room, where she got out her notes and concentrated on studying them. From the notes she turned to the preliminary draft of the article, but after reading it over she tore this first effort to shreds and threw them into the wastepaper basket in disgust. For the rest of the afternoon she typed steadily, revising and re-revising what she had written, trying to shape the potted biography into interesting reading for the ever-curious public. She was only interrupted once, when Bron Pendleton brought tea and a biscuit at mid-afternoon. Thereafter she was left in peace until suddenly glancing at her watch Angie noticed how late it was getting, and gathering her papers together she covered the small portable typewriter and set about changing for supper.

CHAPTER 3

SHE was still turning her afternoon's work over in her mind when she returned from the bathroom and taking out one of her dinner dresses, propped her good leg against the wall in order to have both hands free. The dress, of uncrushable silk jersey, slipped easily over her head. It was a simple gown, scooped at the neck with full bishop sleeves ending in neat bows at her wrists. It relied for attraction on its cut and the pattern of huge orange, lemon and white flowers on a black background. Angelina took a lot of trouble with her make-up and at last stood back to inspect the result.

She frowned as in the full-length mirror she caught sight of her feet. Although the skirt of the dress concealed the plastered leg her foot only partially covered with the cast, left five pink toes exposed in sharp contrast to the black patent pump on her other foot. Suddenly Angie remembered that she had a pair of black nylon pop-socks somewhere in her suitcase. She had put them in to wear with slacks should the weather turn extra cold. With some difficulty she managed to bend and draw one of the socks over her left foot before hobbling once more over to the mirror.

With her bare toes concealed her appearance, she decided, looked vastly improved and she turned with confidence to go and join the others for the evening meal. It was the custom of the family to gather each evening in Julius Pendleton's sitting room for a pre-dinner drink, but Angie was only halfway down the corridor before Bron Pendleton came hurriedly out of her husband's room to meet her.

'Julius has had one of his bad days,' she explained. 'He's having supper in bed, so we won't disturb him. Unfortunately Christine hasn't been in to-day. She rang this morning to tell me her mother was ill and she wouldn't be coming in. It would happen to-day of all days. If she'd been here to give Julius what he calls "one of her workouts" he'd probably be feeling fine by now. As it is he's like a bear with a sore head and it's the annual general meeting of the Women's Institute to-night too. I've absolutely got to be there as I'm treasurer this year. Gordon is at a business dinner, so you and Pablo will have to keep one another company. You'll be all right, won't you?'

While she had been talking, Bron led Angie along to the dining room where Pablo was already sitting at the table in front of a big covered casserole. He got up as his stepmother and Angie appeared and with a 'Give Angelina a sherry,' Bron Pendleton went over to the table and began to serve out the steaming contents on to three plates, leaving her two companions to help themselves to vegetables. She ate her own small portion quickly and getting up excused herself, adding as she hurried to the door, 'Go and see how your father is in about an hour, please, Pablo. I'll try not to be too late. Oh, by the way, there's a trifle on the sideboard and coffee's ready on the hotplate. Don't bother to clear away—it can all be done in the morning.'

The door closed quickly and quietly behind her and across the table Angie was amused to see Pablo's eyebrows raised in comical exaggerated surprise. Then he smiled more naturally, the clownish expression at Bron's hasty departure fading from his face as he met the twinkle Angie could not hide. He forked a mouthful of food into his mouth, then as Angie did not speak remarked, 'Where've you been hiding all afternoon? Surely you're not still annoyed with my father for arranging for you to be seen as a private patient?'

'No, I've been working.' Angie's explanation was brief and to the point. She concentrated on her plate, wishing she had known beforehand that a solitary dinner with Pablo was to be her lot this evening. Then like Julius Pendleton she would have asked to have her meal in bed. Now a whole evening alone with Pablo stretched out before her. She could hardly make her excuses and go off to her room as soon as they finished eating.

She cleared her plate and put her knife and fork neatly side by side, suddenly aware of a curious silence, and glancing up found Pablo regarding her with amusement.

'Not too keen on my undiluted company unless you're busy picking my brain, eh?' he enquired with uncomfortable perception. 'Now I wonder, have you got a guilty secret, or am I not your type?'

Angie reddened. 'What have my personal feelings got to do with you?' she began, aware as the words left her lips that they sounded tactless. 'I just want to get my work here finished and get back home,' she rushed on, miserably aware that she was making bad worse. 'I have a perfectly good flat I share with Netta and we have someone to look after us and get our meals. Your stepmother was under a misapprehension when she thought I'd be unable to cope.'

'I'm well aware of the fact,' Pablo announced calmly as he walked over to the sideboard to return with two dessert plates and the dish of trifle.

'Why didn't you tell her, then? Why let her practically kidnap me from the hospital and say nothing?' Angie demanded, ignoring the fact that she herself could have easily explained her true circumstances to Bron Pendleton at the time of the accident.

'For several reasons,' Pablo answered as he placed a portion of trifle in front of Angie. 'I knew that because of your leg injury I might have to continue the interview in London if you were to finish the magazine article, but if you remained here the situation had distinct possibilities,' and his brown eyes gleamed as he spooned dessert into his mouth.

'Possibilities for what?' There was no smile in Angie's eyes as she pushed back her chair and leaning her weight on the tabletop, got clumsily to her feet. 'Now if you've quite finished wolfing trifle I think I'll have coffee in my bedroom and do some more work.'

But she knew even as she spoke that there was little point in touching the papers in her briefcase. She had cut, revised, changed and re-changed the outline of this, her most elusive subject, and her heart missed a beat as she waited for Pablo to get up and fetch the crutches without which she was helpless to move. But he still sprawled in his chair, silently appraising her, and Angie was suddenly aware of an electric quality in the atmosphere. For all his slight build and lack of height Pablo resembled a coiled spring that might at any moment erupt into unexpected action. His was an insidious masculinity, and Angie found she was trembling as he got very slowly to his feet and walked round the table towards her.

She stood, her hands pressed on the tabletop, and turned unwillingly to meet his eyes. They were only an inch or two higher than her own and she was, she discovered, desperately afraid of what she would read there. But the expression to be seen in Pablo's eyes was by no means intimidating and Angie stood in speechless silence, waiting for him to make the first move.

She hadn't long to wait. He stooped, put one arm round her shoulders, the other under her knees, and lifted her off the ground so that she exploded into instant fury, her fear of him forgotten.

'Put me down at once!' then as disregarding her command he began to carry her towards a buttoned Victorian couch beside the wall Angie said bitterly, 'You're despicable!'

'Am I really? What a superbly antique word. One doesn't hear it much these days. Not "cad" too?'

Angie pressed her lips firmly together and assumed what she hoped was a dignified and at the same time formidable frown. It didn't seem to have the desired effect, for Pablo held her closer and smiled down derisively. 'I fully intend putting you down as soon as possible, my love. You're a clumsy baggage to handle with that thing on your leg, but I could hardly leave you propping up the dining table indefinitely. And I was afraid if I fetched your crutches you might try and give me a wallop with one of them. Now we can sit down and drink our coffee in comfort, or if you like discuss at greater length the permutations that might arise out of your unscheduled stay with the Pendleton family. They could well take up the rest of the evening—among other topics, that is.'

He put her on the couch, propped cushions behind her and went to fetch the coffee tray, putting it on a convenient table. Pablo sat down beside her on the narrow couch. Angelina had sidled over so that she took up most of the room, but as he sat down Pablo gently pushed her back to her original position, saying as he did so, 'Not hurting you, am I?'

Dearly as she would have liked to say yes, he was, Angie reluctantly shook her head in answer to the question, whereupon he laughed, and leaning to pour the steaming black coffee into two cups remarked, 'I'm glad to see you believe in speaking the truth and shaming the devil, however much it goes against the grain. Sugar?' Angie did not reply for a second, bewildered by the sudden change of subject. 'Sweet enough without, I think,' he challenged, then before Angie could anticipate his next move, Pablo suddenly put down the sugar basin and took her into his arms.

Angie twisted her head from side to side to avoid the inevitable kiss, but he simply removed one arm from around her waist and taking her chin in the palm of his hand turned her lips towards his own. She pounded her clenched fists on his unprotected shoulders and chest, but for all the notice he took, she might have saved her strength. Pablo simply held her a little tighter and, unwilling to see the triumph in his eyes, Angie closed her own.

This proved to be her undoing, for in shutting out sight all her other senses seemed to increase tenfold. She became suddenly aware of the faint fresh smell of a good shampoo, the fact that the arm around her, though firm, was holding her tenderly and that the fingers against her face were caressing the skin over her cheekbones, but worst and most important, she was shaken off balance by the drumming of her own excited heart and a feeling as if a red-hot fire was being lit inside every bone in her body. She had been kissed many times before, but never had she been compelled to respond so spontaneously, nor was she conscious of the exact moment when her fighting stopped and she began to use her hands to embrace instead of to do battle.

It was some time later before either Pablo or Angelina spoke again and the coffee in their cups had long since gone cold, when suddenly he lifted his head, gazed into her eyes with dismay, and got up abruptly to exclaim, 'Father! I'd forgotten all about him,' as jumping to his feet he hurried quickly from the room. He was absent for nearly a quarter of an hour, and during his absence Angelina had plenty of time to think over the events of the last hour. With growing dismay she saw clearly where her response to his casual love making might be leading; for casual she knew it to be. She was no beauty, and moreover they had met so very recently that she could only reach one conclusion—her addition to his household had been a godsend to a bored philanderer. He had probably made love to Robinetta after a hard day's work in the same light-hearted way and possibly he had meant as little as he had done this evening with herself. After all, these days nobody attached much importance to a kiss or two. He was not to know that modern though they appeared on the surface, both the Snow sisters were a little old-fashioned at heart, even Robinetta, despite her butterfly existence, hankering after marriage and a conventional relationship.

But after her behaviour this evening Angie knew it would be difficult to persuade Pablo Pendleton of this, and her heart failed her as she waited with tumultuous feelings for his return. But she discovered her apprehensions were needless. When Pablo came in a few minutes later and crossed the room he stood looking down at her, a worried frown on his face. 'Feeling tired, love? You look very pale. I think I ought to get you to bed before Bron comes back. She'll have my hide if she thinks I've overtired you,' and fetching the crutches, he helped Angelina to get to her feet and hobble along the corridor to her room. He seated her on the bed, put the crutches near at hand along with her nightie and dressing-gown, and then asked, 'If I unzip your dress, can you manage alone?'

Angie nodded, her one idea to get rid of him as quickly as possible. She felt his hands at the nape of her neck, the long zipper begin to slide, then the warmth of a kiss on her bare back as a laughing voice remarked, 'Um, you smell delicious. Dior, if I'm not mistaken.'

She watched as the door closed quietly behind him, only to re-open almost immediately. Angie held on to the bodice of her dress as it threatened to slip and was furious to notice Pablo had seen her quick reaction. 'I only came back to ask if you'd like a hot drink. I'm just going to get one for Father.'

Angie shook her head, refusing to respond to the fun in the laughing eyes watching her round the door. 'Right, I'll leave you in peace, then. See you to-morrow, sweetheart. Sleep well,' and the head withdrew.

As Angie got ready for bed, she tried unsuccessfully to reanimate her anger towards Pablo, but it was impossible. What a fool she was being—and this without the complication of her sister's apparently hopeless infatuation for this most unnerving and unpredictable man. Still, Angie thought as she slid carefully between the sheets, there was nothing she could do at the moment to alter the chain of events, and since she was something of a fatalist at heart she put out the light and resolved to let the future take care of itself.

Christine had hardly finished helping Angie to dress the following morning when Pablo's knock was heard at the door. It was a beautiful morning and a little of the day's radiance seemed to enter with him because in a quick, half shamed glance at his face Angie noticed that the glow in his eyes reflected the sunshine out of doors. It seemed that Christine too noticed something different about him, because she remarked jokingly, 'What's up with you this morning, Pablo? You look as if you've just come into a fortune.'

'Don't be inquisitive, and learn to have a little more respect for your elders,' he said playfully as Angie picked up a comb and started to do her hair. Christine was making the bed and she laughed across at him quite unmoved by his mock reprimand. 'You two are taking your time this morning,' Pablo went on, and he leaned against the door jamb and watched the two girls.

'Well, it would be finished a lot quicker if you helped me make this bed,' said Christine. 'Come and tuck in the other side.'

To Angie's astonishment, Pablo walked obligingly across the room and helped Christine make up the bed. Casting a quick eye around to see that everything was in order, Christine went away, saying as she did so, 'You're all right now, aren't you, Angie? I must go and see to Mr. Pendleton,' and the door closed behind her with the words.

As soon as they were alone Pablo walked over to where Angie was sitting and tilting up her face gently kissed her on the lips, saying as he did so, 'Well, I must say you look as if you slept well, chicken.'

Angie's eyelids flickered and then she looked up to meet the bright brown eyes. The hand was still holding her chin. 'Yes, I slept very well, thank you. And you?'

Pablo released her and stood back. 'My, we are being polite this morning, aren't we?' He leaned his shoulders against the wall. 'Couldn't you sound a bit more pleased to see me?' As she didn't reply Pablo went on, 'What are we to do this morning? Any more questions to ask, or have you finally finished?'

'I don't think I've any more to ask you. I've pelted you with questions ever since I came here,' Angie said thoughtfully, 'and I've drafted out the article. It's just a case of doing a little more revising and checking a few details before I send it off to Basil.'

'May I see it, please?'

Angie hesitated for a moment. 'Yes, of course, if you really want to.' She wasn't keen on showing her work to Pablo at this early date, although she know that before it went into print it would have to receive his formal approval.

'Come on, give it to me and we'll go across to the barn. I've left some coffee brewing. I know you've had breakfast, but I daresay you could drink another cup. I can read the article while you have some early elevenses.'

There seemed no reasonable argument to this suggestion, so Angie withdrew the draft article from her briefcase and handed it to Pablo. He pushed it under one arm, leaving both his hands free to help her to the door. In a short while she was seated in her usual chair in the studio, an ancient wing-back which had been recently upholstered, judging by the condition of the leatherwork. He put a cup of coffee in her hand and Angie stirred it thoughtfully as Pablo sat down and began to read her article.

She was completely silent until he had finished the last page and she continued to watch somewhat apprehensively as he shuffled the typescript together again, clipping the pages together and placing them carefully on the table beside him before he looked across and met her eyes. It was impossible to read his expression and she wondered what he was thinking. She didn't have to wait very long to find out.

'A more soulless piece of writing I've yet to see,' he remarked. 'I wouldn't have believed it came from the same pen as those other articles I read before I agreed to let you do a piece about me. There's no warmth, no character, in fact nothing to recommend it, and you make me appear a pompous idiot, almost a cardboard character. Is that really how you see me, Angelina?'

Angie had expected some sort of criticism, but certainly not this, and she was at a loss for words. What could she say in answer to his questions. That he intended to sit in silence and wait for a reply was obvious, for Pablo eyed her with an unwavering stare as she cudgelled her brain for something to say.

'I knew it wasn't as good as the others, but I didn't think it was as bad as that,' she replied at last.

'Frankly it's deplorable. Goodness knows you've pumped me dry the last few days. Surely you must know yourself that it's not a true or accurate picture, even though you did dislike me at the beginning. I'm no saint, but at least I'm alive. In this,' and he tapped the papers contemptuously with his forefinger, 'I read like someone out of a second-rate play—supporting player, and a wooden one at that. Somebody popped into the cast for makeweight, or to give some actor on hard times a part in his old age.'

Angie spurted into laughter. 'And it's no laughing matter,' Pablo went on. 'You can't really imagine I'm going to let *Ladies' Graces* publish this rubbish. Either you do it again and make me sound as if I belong to the human race, or the whole thing's washed out. And you can tell Basil I said so or I will,' he finished. Suddenly he asked quietly, 'What did I do to you, Angie, to merit this sort of treatment? I know you didn't like me at first, but I thought all that was changed, especially after last night.'

Angie flushed slowly. She could feel her face reddening until it felt as if it was on fire, but Pablo didn't seem in a mood to spare her embarrassment, and he didn't take his eyes off her for a second, watching with cruel interest as her face reddened and then slowly went pale again.

'You may well blush,' he said. 'I'm ashamed of you, my girl.'

'I'm *not* your girl!' The words were out almost before Angie could stop them, and immediately Pablo's eyebrows rose alarmingly.

'After reading this that's self-evident,' he said, and getting up he strolled over to the window and stood with his back turned to her, silent for a moment or two before he turned round to face her again. 'I think the best thing is for us to forget the whole thing. I'll have a word with Basil and tell him the accident has really put you off colour and I think the interview ought to be postponed indefinitely.'

'Oh no, don't!' He was altogether too hasty for her peace of mind. 'I'll alter the article if that's what you want.'

Pablo walked slowly back and sat down in his chair. He had a deflated look on his face, Angie thought, and she wondered what was going through his mind. 'I hardly think it's worth it,' he said, and he looked up into her eyes directly. 'I don't think you're in a position to write a truthful article about me, now are you, Angelina?'

Angie found that she was gripping her fingers together in her lap. 'I honestly don't know,' she admitted at last. 'I've written and rewritten that article several times and I don't know why, it just won't come out right.'

At her words Pablo's face softened and getting up he

came across and crouched down by her chair. 'I know we thought of using the accident as an excuse for scrapping the article altogether,' he said, and tucked her fingers between his own, 'but I rather think it really did take more out of you than you realise. That and the fact that somewhere Robinetta's mixed up in all this, isn't she?'

Angelina could think of no reply as she gazed into his eyes, and after staring back for a moment Pablo patted her hand and getting up walked back to his own chair. 'All right, chicken, let's forget it for the moment. We're doing no good having a post-mortem.' He turned his head to look out of the window. 'What do you say we forget all about the wretched business and get the car out? I know a little place about fifty miles from here. It's quiet and you'd enjoy the run. You've been stuck in too much with that leg of yours.'

Pablo's suggestion meant further time alone with him, but anything was better than staying here in futile argument or going back to her bedroom where Bron Pendleton would be pretty sure to come looking for her. Angie reluctantly nodded in agreement to his suggestion and at once Pablo was galvanised into action. Within twenty minutes she found herself comfortably settled in the passenger seat of his car and they were spinning down the drive to turn on to the main road.

'All right?' Pablo enquired. 'Have I put the seat far enough back for your leg to rest comfortably?'

'I'm fine,' Angie said briefly, then added as an afterthought, 'thank you.'

Pablo chuckled. 'Did you find it hard to get that out, my dear one?' he asked, and glanced quickly sideways at her.

Angie smiled, half ashamed of her bad manners. Despite his forthright way of talking she found his underlying good humour hard to withstand. Since his question really required no answer she asked, 'Where are we going?'

'I thought we'd go down to the coast. A breath of sea air will probably do us both good. And I've told Bron we won't be back for supper so brace yourself, you're going to have to spend the entire day with me. I've a packed lunch in the boot.'

He didn't ask if she minded, Angie noticed, and she discovered to her astonishment that she was really quite delighted at his highhandedness. Had she been asked to go out for the day she would have undoubtedly refused the invitation, for she and this astounding man always seemed to end up at odds with one another. The business of the disputed article still hung heavily between them. At least so it seemed to Angelina, although as they travelled swiftly towards the sea Pablo appeared to have dismissed it from his mind. He chatted on about all sorts of topics, from the world political situation to the possibility of England winning the present Test Match, and Angie found herself enjoying the banter without which he never seemed to be able to conduct a conversation. Pablo had an interesting and enquiring mind, she decided, and knew of only one other person with whom she could talk quite so comfortably—her Uncle John.

When Pablo was busy concentrating on his driving Angie unobtrusively studied him, deciding once again that there was little if anything to be discovered by just looking at the outside skin of this man, for it gave no indication at all of the individual within; of the complex character who might be either very bad or the soul of integrity, and she could not decide which, for one moment he repelled her then the next instant confused her by turning on his not inconsiderable charm. She wished he would clear up the matter of Robinetta, for that also hung between them. Angie was the sort of person who liked to have everything spelled out in three-letter words, and there was no doubt that she and Pablo would have to talk things out if she were ever to understand him.

It wasn't a prospect Angie looked forward to with any degree of pleasant anticipation, for she had already discovered that when it came to a sparring match she came off very much the worst. Whatever her arguments, however good her reasoning, he always seemed to be able to find a counter-argument equally strong and often quite unanswerable. Even on impersonal topics he could run rings round her, and this gave her a feeling of faint frustration, despite the fact that Angie had to admit to herself on many occasions that he could well be right. It was bad enough, she thought, to be out-argued, but it was even worse to have the sneaking feeling that one's opponent had done his homework well and was better informed.

As they continued on their way it seemed Pablo was deliberately avoiding built-up areas, for traffic was light, and soon Angie caught a glimpse of the sea ahead. He drove down a narrow track which did not appear to lead anywhere and she was about to ask him if they were lost when she noticed they were approaching a small farmhouse. Pablo drove into the farmyard, stopped the car and with a 'Wait here. I'll be back shortly,' went over to the back door, knocked and waited until the door was opened by a young rosy-cheeked woman wearing a flowered overall. He was back in a few minutes, reversing the car out of the farmyard and continuing on down the track which got narrower and grassier as they proceeded.

When they reached a field gate he stopped and got out to open it, saying as he returned to the car, 'I often come down here. The Griffiths know me well and they don't mind me using their private road as long as I make sure and close the gates.' There was a stile on the far side of the field. 'Not too rough for your leg?' Pablo asked as the car lurched over a particularly uneven patch of ground. Angie, who on seeing the rut ahead had managed to brace herself, shook her head. 'No, it's all right, I didn't feel a thing.'

When they got close to the stile Pablo braked in the

shadow of a leafy hedge and turned off the engine. He sat for a moment gazing straight ahead and then turned to look at Angie. 'Now, I wonder if I can get you over that or not,' he said, and nodded towards the stile.

'It depends how high it is. I certainly can't climb over with this wretched plaster on my leg.'

'No, but if you can manage to balance on the top rail I expect I could swing you down on the other side. It's well worth the exercise if we can do it without hurting you. Anyway, stay here a moment. I'll go and investigate.'

Opening the car door Pablo got out and walked over to the stile. 'Fine, it's much lower than I thought. One minute while I get the gear out,' he called as he walked behind to open the boot. A few minutes later he passed Angie's window carrying a folding chair, a rug and a bulging carrier bag.

He disappeared over the stile quickly returning to open her door. 'Leave your crutches where they are. You won't need them,' he ordered, and reaching in he eased her carefully into his arms. When they reached the stile Pablo rested her gently on the top bar which fortunately was broad and strong then hopping nimbly over he picked her up again.

'Now that was fairly easy, Princess, wasn't it?' he asked as he walked towards the spot where he had left the chair ready for her occupancy. There was even a cushion on it, she noticed as he put her down carefully and then spread out the rug and sitting down himself began to rummage in the bag of food. He produced a thermos of coffee, two mugs and a big plastic-wrapped package which he opened to reveal a pile of succulent-looking ham sandwiches. He held them up to Angie who took one.

'I didn't think you'd want a lot to eat at this stage,' he said. 'We'll have an early dinner, okay?'

'Suits me,' Angie replied, and wondered at her own meek acquiescence as she gazed out to where, not very far below her, the ground shelved away towards a deserted shingly beach. The sun was beginning to come out from behind a bank of cloud and the sea sparkled as it rippled over the pebbles. There wasn't a soul about, although on the still air she could hear the sound of a farm tractor being driven somewhere in the fields behind her.

'Pleasant here, don't you think?' Pablo asked. 'It's my favourite spot to come if I want to think and be quite alone.'

'Don't you ever bring anyone for company?' Angie's tones were sceptical.

'Never before to-day.' Pablo turned to look at Angie with a distinctly teasing gleam in his eyes. 'Dad gave up going on picnics long ago for obvious reasons and of course Bron won't have a day out without him. Gordon's never been the sporty type. He likes central heating and lots of parties, the countryside leaves him cold. A game of golf's about his only outdoor pursuit. Now I like to get out here now and again to really breathe the fresh air. I've even tried to sketch this bay on one or two occasions, though without much success. Somehow or other I can't capture the beauty. It *is* beautiful, isn't it? Don't you agree?'

Angie nodded dreamily. 'Yes. Gorgeous! London with its smoke and busy streets seems a million miles away. Sometimes I wonder how I stand it. I hate the thought on an afternoon like this of having to go back.'

'Me too,' Pablo agreed, 'but it's back to the treadmill for me next week.'

'Another assignment on the cards?' Angie asked.

'Something like that,' Pablo nodded. 'Anyway, I understand that people are screaming about one or two bits of business I rather left in the air when I came away, so I'll have to get back to work. Pity really. I was enjoying this stay down in Wales rather more than I usually do,' and he cocked an eyebrow as he looked up into Angie's face.

She flushed and looked away towards the sea. 'Now why

the pretty blush on this occasion?' he quizzed her. 'Don't you like men to flatter you?'

Angie was silent for a moment before she turned and looked down into the brown eyes smiling guilelessly up at her. How could one harden one's heart against a man like this? At every turn he disarmed her so that she found herself responding to him against her better judgement. The spectre of Robinetta faded as Angie gazed down into Pablo's eyes, and although she was unaware, her own eyes began to light up in response to the smile in his.

'That's better,' he nodded, and his smile broadened. 'I was beginning to think that having just found the girl of my dreams last night, she'd faded from view again this morning. But I can see I was wrong. We were meant for each other, don't you know that?'

His face was suddenly serious and Angie drew in her breath sharply. He couldn't mean what he was saying, she thought for a moment, and her smile faded. Suddenly she couldn't face the confrontation she had so earnestly desired, afraid that it might spoil their beautiful transient communion. There might never be another occasion when they were at peace with each other as now. 'It's a lovely day and we're enjoying it together. Don't let's start analysing our relationship yet,' she pleaded.

Pablo's eyes searched her face keenly for a moment and then he nodded. 'All right, it shall be as you wish, my dear girl. No arguments, no recriminations and no decisions. We'll play it one minute at a time if that's what you want.'

Angie wasn't aware that she let out a huge breath of relief and relaxed deeply into her chair, but Pablo, watching her keenly, saw the release of tension and wondered what was passing through her mind. Angie could easily have told him, but she was being a coward, pushing the problems which in due course would have to be faced away from her. She was playing the ostrich, burying her head in the sand—almost literally, she thought, with the beach at her feet, pebbly though it was. She wished she could float away this very minute with the pleasant feeling that all was right with her world and never have to come back. She didn't want to face rewriting the interview, Robinetta's entanglements, or anything else for that matter, and wished that this quiet limbo could go on for ever. She knew in her heart of hearts that it couldn't, but with Pablo's co-operation perhaps for a day or two she could ignore the many obstacles which stood between them. Pretend they had met without prejudice to warp her judgement.

Pablo, as if he sensed her withdrawal, spent the rest of the afternoon talking about quite impersonal matters and keeping her amused until they reached the small inn where he had arranged for them to eat their evening meal. It was very tiny and the dining room was almost full, the clientèle consisting mostly, Angie guessed, of farmers and their wives and families, for the other diners had not the pale skins or appearance of townspeople and the menu card was brief, giving little choice. It offered soup or grapefruit as a first course followed by steak and kidney pie or cold meat and salad. There were no desserts listed at all.

As she put the small card down again Angie glanced across to see that Pablo's eyes were dancing. 'Not exactly the Ritz,' he said, 'but the cooking here is out of this world—if you like plain British fare, that is. Now I wouldn't recommend the grapefruit. It's nearly always tinned. Have the soup.'

'On a day like this?' Angie protested, and glanced out of the window where the sun was still shining despite the fact that it was after seven in the evening.

'Yes, in spite of the warm weather. And although the cold buffet will be perfect, I recommend the steak and kidney pie. There's no need to have potatoes. You can have two green vegetables if you like or a salad on the side.'

A quarter of an hour later as she sipped the clear soup Angie decided Pablo's advice had been excellent. The soup had obviously been made of good juicy bones and there was a piquant flavour of some added wine and herbs to which she found it impossible to put a name. She spooned up the last drop and put her spoon down, glancing up to meet Pablo's eyes.

'What did I tell you?' he smiled, and indicated his own empty plate. 'I've never tasted soup anywhere, not even in London, that's like this. Now wait until you get a sight of the steak and kidney pie.'

Angie gasped at the enormous portion put down in front of her and protested that she'd never manage to get through it. As he helped her to cauliflower liberally covered with a rich cheese sauce and a portion of fresh peas, Pablo brushed aside her protests with a brusque, 'Nonsense, girl, stop quibbling and get stuck into it,' as he helped himself to lavish helpings from the vegetable dishes.

Once again Angie discovered that he was right, for she didn't have much difficulty in tucking away the feathery pastry, the beautifully cooked steak and kidney and those equally delicious vegetables. But when at last her plate was cleared she sat back and looked across the table at Pablo. 'I shall burst, I'm sure I shall,' she announced in unladylike tones.

'Don't worry, you'll be in good company,' said Pablo, patting his own abdomen. 'Now all we shall be offered is cheese, biscuits and coffee. They serve no sweets here.'

'I couldn't eat another thing,' Angie protested, but her protests were disregarded as the waitress took away their plates, put down butter, biscuits and a wooden board containing three large slabs of cheese.

'Not a lot to choose from,' Pablo commented, 'but very good none the less. The customers round here won't touch what they call "them foreign cheeses," so there's only

Caerphilly, Cheshire and Cheddar. Come on, take your choice,' and he wouldn't hear of Angelina refusing.

She ate one small biscuit with a morsel of Caerphilly cheese and watched dismayed as the waitress returned with huge breakfast cups of steaming black coffee and a jug of fresh cream, which she set down on the table at their elbows.

'Don't look so horrified,' Pablo laughed. 'You can take your time over this. Why not have a cigarette and keep me company?'

'I've never smoked,' Angie confessed.

'What? Not even when you were at school?'

'No, not even then,' she replied. 'I've never had the urge one way or another—perhaps it was because Mother and Father were non-smokers.'

'Strange, one seldom comes across a whole family who don't smoke. Robinetta never touches them either, does she?'

Angelina decided that Pablo had dropped the name into the conversation deliberately and so she answered firmly, 'No, she's never smoked as far as I know,' and immediately turned the conversation by enquiring how he had discovered the inn and how long the restaurant had been going. If Pablo noticed her unwillingness to continue discussing Robinetta he gave no sign and answered in a commonplace manner, saying that he and Gordon had heard about the place two years earlier, but it was a bit too rustic for Gordon's taste and after one visit he had not returned.

'But I bring Bron here sometimes and Christine and I have had a meal up here once or twice,' he confessed. 'I'd sooner have two really well-cooked choices than an enormous menu where sometimes one wonders how often the food has been re-heated, and it's such a welcome relief after the stuffy London restaurants. I have to eat out when I'm up there. I don't have any living in help and though I can get my own breakfast I'm not much of a cook other than of the bacon and egg variety. Like you, I don't bother very much about lunch, I have a beer and a sandwich as a rule and get on with what I'm doing. But in the evening I tend to go out rather a lot to have a decent feed, and of course I've got to entertain in the line of business.'

Angie's eyes began to twinkle. 'All those glamorous models. Do they have to be kept sweet sometimes by a dinner at the Savoy?'

'Oh, not the Savoy,' said Pablo. 'Most of them prefer somewhere much more out of the way. They go for these intimate restaurants which are springing up all over the place. And usually for some exotic type of food too. They think it square to eat good old British food. I can't tell you the number of Chinese, Indian and other kinds of culinary art I've had to sample just to keep some capricious dolly in an amenable frame of mind.'

Angelina couldn't help wondering if one of the capricious ladies might not have been her own sister. Perhaps this was the answer she was seeking. Perhaps in order to keep her sweet and reasonable Pablo had taken her out sufficiently often to make Robinetta imagine that his interest was personal. Perhaps she had read a great deal more into what Pablo said and did than he had actually intended. But Angie had decided earlier that she wasn't going to spoil what had turned out to be a happy day and she pushed these thoughts resolutely away to get the conversation back on to topics which would neither remind her of her sister nor of the fact that now she knew she was falling headlong in love with a man she had been sure she would detest.

It had taken him little more than three weeks to turn her world upside down. Instead of feeling her usual poised, sure and capable self she was behaving more like an eighteen-year-old indulging in her first love affair, and instead of firm ground beneath her feet Angie sensed quicksands ahead becoming more dangerous day by day. She recalled the old saying about 'the path of true love' and grimaced over this unhappy thought as Pablo helped her to the car.

They returned to the Pendleton home just after ten o'clock and instead of going straight in Pablo suggested a last cup of coffee in the barn studio before going to bed. He carried her in from the car and put her into the wing-back chair.

'Did you enjoy the day?' he asked as he released her.

Angie looked up at him. How brown he looked! The day in the sunshine had added to his quite considerable tan, and against it the brown eyes seemed even brighter. Pablo bent, put a hand on each arm of the chair and kissed her gently on the end of her nose. 'I can see you did, Princess. Good! A day out takes your mind off things better left unsaid,' he remarked, and before she could answer he turned away and walked over to where the coffee things were kept. His remark required no answer, Angelina decided, but she sighed faintly as she sat back in the chair. How nice it would have been if she and Pablo could have met under different circumstances without any of the shadows which already she could see lying ahead.

The next two days followed almost exactly the same pattern. Nothing was said about the interview. Angelina made no attempt to work and she and Pablo spent all day in each other's company either in the barn or on some expedition to a local beauty spot. If Bron and Julius Pendleton noticed a change in the pattern of Angie's day they made no reference to her long absences from the house, nor to the length of time which they spent in Pablo's studio barn. Perhaps, she thought, they merely assumed she was continuing her investigations for the article she was writing.

It was on the fourth afternoon when Pablo and Angie were about to go and have tea in Julius Pendleton's sitting room that the sound of a car coming rapidly up the drive reached their ears. It braked sharply, a door slammed and quick footsteps were heard coming over to the barn. They both looked towards the door as it swung open, to discover Robinetta in the doorway poised to catch and hold their full attention like an actress making her first entrance in a play.

She looked assured and beautiful in slimly cut summer slacks, a blouse in fine patterned cotton with billowing sleeves and a loose suede jacket which exactly matched the colouring of her trousers. She walked straight across the barn to fling herself upon Pablo's chest and ask in an emotional voice, 'Why didn't you tell me you were down here? Why have I been kept in the dark about Angie's visit? Darling, I've been so worried. Why haven't you been in touch with me?'

Whether it was by instinct or merely a reflex action Pablo's hands came up and rested on Robinetta's shoulders and to Angie watching from her chair the sight of Robinetta in his arms was insupportable. Tears blinded her eyes as she groped for her crutches and struggled to her feet.

'Don't go,' Pablo said quickly, but already Angelina had turned towards the door. Making no effort to disengage herself, Robinetta looked over her shoulder, her arms still clasped about Pablo's neck. 'Pablo and I have a lot to say to one another. I'll see you later,' she said in an aggressive tone as, hardly able to see where she was, Angie hobbled away.

The moment of reckoning had come and her few days of self-delusion were over. Now she would have to face reality, and as she went towards the house to slip in through a side door she admonished herself for her cowardice in not doing so earlier. If only she had faced up to things at the start instead of letting herself go with the current this hurtful moment might have been prevented. That Pablo was in some way committed she had known from the first, but she hadn't realised that Robinetta's claim was apparently so strong. He had not repulsed her sister's affectionate greeting, nor had he made any genuine attempt to stop Angie's exit, so there could only be one answer to this sort of behaviour. Robinetta's statement that Pablo had asked her to marry him must be true, despite his conduct during the last three days.

Angelina was making her way along the downstairs corridor when she met Bron Pendleton pushing the tea trolley. 'Pablo not coming in for tea?' she asked as they met.

Angie stopped and leaned her weight on her crutches. 'Pablo has a visitor. My sister, as a matter of fact.'

Bron looked surprised. 'I had no idea he'd met your sister.' She looked thoughtfully at Angie as she spoke, and her curiosity was plain to see.

'She's one of his models; I thought you knew,' Angie lied, and determined now to avoid the curious stares of the other members of the household when Robinetta was introduced added, 'Would you think me very unsociable if I took a cup of tea into my room and did some work? I've got a bit behind the last few days and must get on.'

'Of course not,' Bron answered immediately, and began to pour out the tea. 'Here, let me take it in. Can you manage the door?'

Angie nodded and turned away as Bron followed her with the tea. 'Sure you won't have some cake or a biscuit?' Bron enquired as she put the cup and saucer on the desk, and Angie smiled and shook her head as she sat down thankfully in an easy chair. 'In that case, we'll see you at supper,' Bron said. 'I'll not let anyone disturb you meantime if you want to work. I know how annoyed Julius gets if anyone pops in and out when he and Christine have really got their teeth into it.'

Angie knew by now Julius Pendleton had found a new vocation writing textbooks after polio had put an end to his career as an engineer and that Christine, as well as helping with the nursing he required, also doubled as secretary, typing his manuscripts. He usually worked solidly until lunchtime every day and this was one of the reasons why Pablo had originally forbidden photographs of the rear of the house and garden.

Angie sipped her tea slowly. How she had misjudged him over that, thinking he had just been manufacturing difficulties because he did not wish to co-operate over the interview. She opened her briefcase and taking out the article which she had written she re-read it, this time with a more impartial eye. How right he had been to condemn it! This was a piece of journalism utterly without warmth or merit, and she ought to be thoroughly ashamed of herself. A good writer should always approach each new subject with a completely open mind. Not only did the piece lack life, but she could see now a bias which she had not intended to express and which as a professional writer she should have overcome.

Angie tore the pages into tiny pieces and dropped them into the wastepaper basket, then taking out fresh paper, she inserted it into her small portable typewriter. More than two hours passed before she stopped, gathered up the sheets of typescript and making sure they were in numerical order clipped them together. She had addressed an envelope to Basil Beavis and was licking a stamp when Christine Casement put her head round the door.

'Do you know what time it is?' Christine asked. 'The others are having a drink in Mr. Pendleton's room and I think they're waiting for you. I'm just off. Anything I can do before I go?'

Angie glanced at her wristwatch. She had not known how late it was getting. 'Goodness, I hadn't realised the time.' She smiled across at Christine. 'The only thing I'd like is to get this posted,' she held up the bulky envelope. 'Do you go near a post box? If it's not out of your way, that is.'

But even as she spoke Angie hoped Christine would take the package so that she could have no more second thoughts. If she kept it only until the morning she might be tempted to change what she felt at this moment was at least a creditable and, she hoped, perceptive biography. It would be one problem out of the way; the second and more important, Robinetta's unexpected arrival, she must face in a few minutes, and there wasn't much time to prepare herself for the more difficult hurdle.

Angie got changed in record time, brushed her hair until it shone, applied a minimum of make-up and went along to Julius Pendleton's sitting room. He and his wife were over by the window sipping sherry, while on the settee, her hand tucked possessively through Pablo's arm, sat Robinetta. How beautiful she looks, Angie thought as Pablo disengaged himself to get up and help her to a chair. He did not resume his place when he had supplied Angie with a drink, but went over to an easy-chair, whereupon Robinetta immediately got up to sit beside him on the arm of the chair. She had changed into a sea green silk halter-neck dinner dress, which showed off her Mediterranean tan to great advantage. Her eyes sparkled and she was obviously in the best of spirits, even Julius Pendleton, not the most susceptible of men, responding to her charm and gaiety.

Pablo was refilling their glasses when Gordon Pendleton pushed open the door, saying as he did so, 'Sorry I'm late.' At once he noticed the newcomer perched on the arm of the big easy-chair and Angie saw his eyes widen. 'Introduce me, someone,' he demanded, and Pablo turned to say, 'Robinetta, meet my brother. I don't have to tell you this lovely lady is one of our leading models, do I, Gordon? She is also Angie's sister, hence her unexpected arrival.'

By this time Gordon was holding Robinetta's small

hand and smiling down into her eyes, the surprised delight still apparent in his own. 'You are a dark horse,' he said at length across the room to Angelina, reluctantly releasing her sister's hand as Pablo handed him a glass. 'You never mentioned being related to this gorgeous creature. Why haven't we met before this?' he asked Robinetta.

Angie's eyes were sad as she watched the scene being played out before her. That Gordon neither expected an answer to his question nor was really aware of the rest of the family, Angie could see with the eyes of experience. Not one of the men dazzled by Robinetta's extraordinary good looks ever seemed to worry that she had little or no brains. Intelligence was rarely an acceptable exchange for beauty in a man's eyes, Angie knew. It was a bitter lesson she had learned and accepted as soon as Netta was old enough to leave school.

But one person in the room had not focused his whole attention on the latest guest. As she looked away from Robinetta's laughing face, Angie discovered that Pablo was leaning back against the drinks cabinet and that he was watching her closely. The moment her eyes met his own he walked over to her chair and bending down whispered, 'Why did you disappear? I came to look for you, but Bron said you didn't want to be disturbed. Not feeling ill or anything?'

'Of course not,' Angie smiled faintly. 'I thought you and Netta would have lots to talk about. I'd only have been in the way, so I went to my room to do some work. If you haven't forgotten, I'm supposed to be down here professionally and not just on a leisurely holiday.'

'How can I forget you're not on holiday with that to remind me?' and he indicated her plastered leg, about which Angie suddenly realised Netta hadn't yet troubled to enquire. 'But you don't mean to tell me you are still trying to write a piece about me,' his eyes were satirical.

'You're beaten before you start, like a man trying to teach his wife to drive.'

He walked away with these words and Angie stared thoughtfully after him. Hope flickered to life within her, then died as quickly when Robinetta got up from the chair and slipping her arm through Pablo's, drew him towards the window where they exchanged some low-voiced conversation. They were still whispering together when Bron Pendleton rose and said, 'I think supper should be ready now. Wheel your father into the dining room, please, Gordon. His new chair's had to go for some mechanical adjustments and I refuse to let him use the one he had his accident in.'

Julius sighed and gave his wife a speaking glance as Gordon took hold of the back of his wheelchair and began to push him across the room. Angie scrambled to her feet and followed, determined not to have to accept help from Pablo, and by the time he and Robinetta entered the dining room, Gordon Pendleton had installed his father at the head of the table and pulled a chair out for Angelina on his father's right hand.

As soon as she was comfortably settled he hurried round the table and slid into the seat beside Robinetta, leaving Pablo to take the last empty place. Netta was in her element, Angie noticed, already, from the gleam in her eye, planning how she would play one admirer off against another. But during the meal, Pablo was palpably unresponsive, so that she was forced to concentrate her considerable charm on Gordon Pendleton alone, a situation which appeared to please him very well.

What her host and his wife were thinking Angelina could only guess. Bron was her usual cheerful, hospitable self, urging everyone to generous helpings of the beautifully cooked meal. Julius, while taking part in the general conversation and teasing Robinetta once or twice, concentrated on his food so that on several occasions Angie found herself in a pool of silence between the father on her left and his elder son on her right. It looked like being a difficult evening, she decided, but on returning to the sitting room, Bron turned on the television and soon everyone, even Robinetta, was silent as they drank their after-dinner coffee and watched an unusually gripping drama unfolding on the small screen.

When she was ready for bed Angie provided herself with a book, knowing that Robinetta would be certain to look in later. She was beginning to feel drowsy and wishing her sister would come to bed when Robinetta entered the room in a foaming creation in deep blue chiffon. She was wearing an astonishing full-length nightdress and matching negligée so beribboned and covered with frills that it should have been ridiculous, but instead made her look ravishingly elegant. Seeing the amazement in her sister's eyes Robinetta stood still an instant, then pirouetted to make the fine filmy fabric swirl out in a huge arc round her feet as she turned. 'Like it?' she enquired.

'Wherever did you get it?' Angie asked, amazement still on her face, but she couldn't help smiling as her sister, satisfied she had created a diversion, walked over and settled herself on the end of the bed.

'Oh, I did some work about a month ago for a French lingerie manufacturer,' Robinetta explained. 'I found this waiting for me at the flat when I got home from Sardinia. Now, Angie, what are you up to? I had to positively worm out of Wilkie where you were. And you could have knocked me down with a feather when she told me you'd broken your leg saving Pablo's father and moreover were staying with the Pendletons. Why didn't you write? I'd have come home at once. What better opening for me to get properly established in the family than being the sister of the heroine of the hour?'

Angie winced inwardly. Why had Robinetta to belittle her in this manner? Not that she had done anything particularly heroic. Anyone else seeing Julius Pendleton's predicament would have done their best to prevent an accident, and it was her own fault that she had fallen so clumsily and come off with a broken leg. Still, it seemed unfair that Robinetta should make her sound an interfering do-gooder. It wasn't the first time Robinetta had made her feel ridiculous, but this time for some reason it was different.

His sister was rattling on and Angie forced herself to listen. 'When we were in Venice together you never told me you'd be meeting Pablo when you got home. I suppose you told him we were sisters. What did he say about me?'

'I didn't tell you I was coming down here,' Angie replied wearily, 'because at the time I didn't know. It wasn't until I got back to London that Basil broke the news to me that I was to interview Pablo here in Llantarwyn, and apart from talking about you as one of his many models Pablo hasn't mentioned you in any other context. *I* certainly didn't want to bring you into our conversation, particularly after what you'd told me.'

'But didn't you ask him anything about his feelings for me?' Robinetta demanded.

'It's hardly my business, is it?' Despite herself, Angie knew she was beginning to sound impatient. 'What you and Pablo decide between yourselves about marrying has absolutely nothing to do with me.'

'Just the same,' Robinetta's beautiful mouth was beginning to turn down at the corners, 'I think you might have cabled me as soon as you had the accident and told me that the Pendletons had insisted on your moving in here. You're quite the heroine, you know. The family are loud in their praises of how quickly you acted to save Pablo's father. I must say, though, knowing how I felt, I can't understand why you accepted.'

'They gave me no excuse to refuse, and it seemed a good

opportunity to finish the interview,' Angie replied, and knew she was evading the entire truth. 'I was right in the middle of it when I broke my leg.'

'Well, you seem to be getting about fairly well now, and if you've finished the article I don't see any point in you hanging around any longer. What do you say I run you to the station in the morning and you can catch a train back to London? I'm sure Basil wants you for other work and Wilkie can meet your train.'

Even knowing Robinetta's simple reasoning as she did Angie was silent with sheer astonishment at her naïve suggestion. 'You mean you expect me to simply pack and leave while you stay on?'

'I don't see why not.'

'Well, I imagine the Pendletons would think us both mad. Quite apart from the fact that I've another appointment at the hospital coming up, if I did decide to return to London surely you realise the Pendletons would expect you to drive me there.'

Angelina looked directly across at her sister and noticed that Robinetta avoided meeting her eyes. 'I don't see why they should,' Angie's younger sister sounded sulky. 'After all, they've been told now that I've known Pablo for ages and it won't be long before they guess...!' She stopped and Angie waited for her to finish, but Robinetta, went off on to another tack. 'Well, if you won't go I'm staying too.'

'There's no reason why you shouldn't,' Angie was tired of arguing. 'By all means stay, then you can return to Town with Pablo; he says he must be back by Monday or Tuesday. That way you'd get him entirely to yourself and I can stay and see the specialist as arranged. If you pack me off to London in the morning you'll defeat your object, because I know Pablo has to see to some business in London.'

At her words Robinetta visibly brightened. 'Oh, if that's

the case there's nothing to it. Pablo and I can spend a nice long week-end here together, and then go back to Town in my car on Monday or Tuesday. I'll see him about it first thing in the morning. Goodnight,' and she flounced out of the room without giving her sister a chance to contribute anything further to the conversation.

Angie sighed as the door closed and laying her book on the small table by the bed switched out the reading light. Had Robinetta become more self-centred and vain, or was it her imagination? Angie had always counted on Robinetta's inner warmth and sisterly affection, which she had thought could never be overcome, but she hadn't banked on becoming the object of Robinetta's jealousy. With rare insight Netta had sensed that there was a rapport between Angie and Pablo the moment she made her dramatic appearance, and she was obviously going to use every means at her disposal to destroy it.

CHAPTER 4

NOT that she would have much difficulty in doing so, Angie thought next morning when Robinetta easily persuaded Pablo to take her out for the day. After an abortive attempt to get Angie alone in the studio Pablo made no objection to Robinetta's suggestions and allowed himself to be coaxed into going on a picnic. Neither of them suggested to Angie that she join the expedition, and she watched rather sadly as Pablo wrapped a rug around her sister in the passenger seat of his open car, much as he had done for her on other occasions. Angie turned from the window, unable to watch as they sped away down the drive leaving her to face a long lonely day unrelieved by the return of a laughing twosome, flushed and hungry after a day in the open.

Robinetta monopolised the conversation during the evening meal with tales of what they had done and seen during the day as if she wished to rub salt into the wound, Angie thought, as she sat silently pushing the food around on her plate. She was glad when she could make an excuse to have an early night, saying that she had some work to finish. Only Robinetta knew that she had in fact completed the article, so her explanation seemed natural to the rest of the Pendleton family. When Bron came along later to see if Angelina would like a nightcap she said, 'Pablo and your sister are talking of returning to London on Monday. You don't have to go too, do you?'

'Not if you don't mind having me around and inflicting myself on the household until after I've seen Mr. Richards again.'

Bron cut her short. 'Let's have no more talk about being a nuisance, my dear. Julius and I are only too glad to have you for as long as you can stay. I'm really glad you've got to see the specialist next week, because that means you won't run away too. I was hoping that Pablo would stay a little longer, but unfortunately he tells me he's some work he must attend to.'

Angie smiled and turned the conversation by thanking Bron for looking in. She didn't want to answer questions and seeing that she was able to manage to get undressed Bron said 'Goodnight' and went away. But when her light was out Angie couldn't sleep, and she faced the fact there were going to be more of these nights when all she could do was lie in the darkness and wonder exactly where Pablo was and who he was with. To-night of course she was under no misapprehensions. He was almost certainly at this very moment being walked round the warm perfumed garden by her designing young sister. Had he any intention of marrying her or not? Or was he merely amusing himself with a pretty girl? It was a question which Angie couldn't answer and she turned over on her side and tried desperately to get to sleep.

Before he left on Monday morning Pablo came unexpectedly into the bedroom while Angie was eating her breakfast. 'I'm sorry I've got to rush away like this,' he said without preamble, 'but I'll try and get down again next week-end. Bron says you're seeing Richards on Friday afternoon.'

'Yes, that's right. I'm hoping he'll take the plaster off for good.' Angie was happy to keep the conversation on safe ground.

'We haven't seen much of each other the last day or two,' Pablo pressed on, and Angie realised that he at least was not prepared to fence with her.

In that case, neither would she. 'No, Robinetta's pretty demanding.' Angie looked up and met his eyes directly.

Pablo stared back for a moment. 'Yes,' he answered at last. 'Pity she had to descend on us just now. It rather complicates things.' He glanced at his watch. 'Well, Princess, got to be off, I'm afraid. Be seeing you,' and he turned to walk out of the room.

Angie stared at the closed door, her appetite quite gone. Was he, as Robinetta had suggested when they were in Venice, just not the marrying kind? A born philanderer, perhaps. Robinetta herself had flirted with his brother on the night of her arrival and he might be playing her at her own game. But this was contrary to all Angie had learned about Pablo's character since she had been obliged to accept his father's hospitality. 'But are you much of an authority on men?' an inner voice asked, and Angie sighed as she pushed the bed-tray away wishing that Christine would come and help her get dressed. She needed something which would banish the miserable conflicting thoughts jostling around in her mind.

It seemed very quiet after Pablo and Robinetta had driven away, but fortunately the morning's post brought a thick envelope from *Ladies' Graces* with all the appropriate material on Angelina's next 'victim,' so once dressed she settled in an easy chair and concentrated on the contents of the folder which the research team had sent down. She had never met actor Stuart Blair, now best known by the public for his television series as a gay man-about-town, prone to getting involved in intriguing situations.

In real life he was married to a famous dancer, so there was plenty of homework for Angelina to do and she managed to fill in the following two days by going through the mass of information sent down by her London colleagues. Basil Beavis had enclosed a letter in which he said he wasn't quite certain when Blair would be available for interview as he was at present in Cumberland with his family. It was on the cards that again she and Jack

Bryant would have to go out of town in order to do the interview, but Angelina wasn't sorry to read this piece of news. She did not know Pablo's plans, but since he had already told her he had commitments in London it was possible he would be there for some weeks and meeting him would be unavoidable.

It was not going to be easy to watch her and Robinetta together with his gentleness and lovemaking prior to her sister's unexpected arrival still fresh in her mind. Angelina cursed the fate which had made Basil Beavis choose him above all other photographers to be included in the series for the magazine. There were any number of well-known photographers he could have picked and it was just sheer bad luck that Basil had decided to interview the very man embroiled in an affair with her capricious sister.

On Friday Bron Pendleton drove Angie to the hospital for her appointment with the orthopaedic surgeon. Although Mr. Richards was pleased with the progress which her leg was making and had the old plaster removed for X-rays to be taken he insisted that healing was not sufficiently advanced for Angie to go without a plaster, and much to her disgust had a new one applied before she left.

When it came to the question of another appointment Angelina explained that she would have to be getting back to London.

'In that case give me the name and address of your doctor,' Mr. Richards requested. 'I'll write and explain exactly what we've done so far and then he can refer you to one of the London hospitals. I should think next time you have the plaster off the leg it will be okay. But I daren't take a chance to-day,' and he held her X-rays up to the light. 'At least another fortnight, I'd say. Don't worry, you'll soon have two good legs again. I suppose it's a bit of a nuisance, isn't it?' and he smiled sympathetically.

'You can say that again,' Angelina sighed as she reached

for her crutches and got to her feet with the help of the pretty nurse who had been chaperoning her during her interview. 'The worst part is not being able to get about unaided. I'm an independent soul.'

They were just about to sit down to supper that evening when Bron looked up in surprise as Pablo walked through the dining-room door. 'Good heavens, I thought you'd be fixed in London for some time. We weren't expecting you back so soon, were we, Julius?'

Julius Pendleton looked up to glance enigmatically from his son's face and then across the table at Angelina's, but he made no response to his wife's enquiry and she rattled on as she pushed back her chair. 'Well, come along, sit down. I'll get another plate—there's plenty of cold meat and salad. We've got the Bristows coming in afterwards for bridge. They wouldn't come for a meal.'

Pablo pulled out a chair and groaned. 'In that case I think Angie and I'll escape to the barn. I never could stand the Bristows. I can't think why you invite them.'

'We have to occasionally,' his father replied. 'Old Bristow may be a bit of a bore, but he's a very good solicitor, and remember we went to school together. Anyway, he plays a good hand of bridge.'

'Yes, and when you two start talking of the old school tie it's time we youngsters left,' Pablo gently chided him as he started to load a plate with slices of ham and cold roast beef before helping himself liberally to salad and savoury rice. He was adding horseradish sauce to the mustard on the side of his plate before he looked across and spoke directly to Angelina.

'How's the leg coming along? Was Alex Richards pleased with your progress when you went to see him?'

'Pleased, yes,' said Angelina, 'but willing to take the plaster off, no.' She stretched out her stiff leg. 'As you can see, I'm still a member of the Cripples' Guild.'

Pablo grinned. He didn't seem unduly perturbed by the

fact that Angelina was still literally tied by the leg. 'Well, at least it keeps you in one place,' he said, 'so we all know where you are. No wondering what you're getting up to half the time.'

'Don't be so sure. I can be pretty nifty on these crutches,' Angie retorted, and discovered her voice sounded breathless. She stopped short a moment before she went on and gripped her hands together in her lap. It was ridiculous to be so pleased that Pablo had turned up as he had promised. She had half expected him to return bringing Robinetta with him, but it seemed this had not been his intention, and she was shaken as she considered this unexpected move.

How good it was to see him sitting opposite her at the other side of the dining table, and how fortunate that she had allowed Bron and Julius Pendleton to persuade her to extend her visit another couple of days. She had told them that Mr. Richards was quite willing for her treatment to be continued in London and that she should be getting back to organise her next assignment, but after some discussion it had been provisionally decided that Angie should travel up the following Monday morning and Jack Bryant had promised to meet the train at Euston. There was a good through train from the nearest railhead and Bron had already arranged her Monday morning commitments so she would be free to run her to the station.

But with Pablo's arrival, Angie thought to herself as Bron served the dessert, things might be different. If he had to be back in London on Sunday or Monday, perhaps they could travel together. She would have at least five or six hours of his undiluted company, and she couldn't help the involuntary upward curve of her mouth as she bent over her plate. When she looked up Pablo was watching her. 'A penny for them,' he offered.

Angelina smiled across the table, quite unable to hide the warmth in her eyes. 'Not worth a penny, I'm afraid.

Not even an old one,' and to try and stop his questions she asked him whether it had been hot and stuffy in London.

'Oh, quite intolerable,' Pablo answered. 'We've been having a minor heatwave and London's been like an oven. Fumes from exhausts were so unbearable it was a relief to breathe some clean Welsh air when I got over the border.'

He scraped up the last morsels on his plate and gave a sigh of satisfaction. 'My goodness Bron, that was good,' he said. 'You do a marvellous cold buffet. No four-star hotel could produce anything half as good.' That his stepmother was pleased with his praise Angelina could see, although she made light of it and pretended she thought Pablo was after something because he was complimenting her.

'Now what do you want?' she asked jokingly. 'You don't usually make remarks about my cooking.'

Pablo pretended to be hurt. 'Aren't women marvellous, Dad?' he asked, and looked towards his father. 'Pay them a compliment and immediately they think you've got some ulterior motive!'

Julius Pendleton laughed. 'I've never met one yet who didn't,' he remarked.

'Impossible creatures, men,' Bron said as she began to clear away the used plates, 'and they stick together, what's more.'

Everybody started to laugh as she piled the supper things on to the trolley. Refusing cheese and biscuits, Pablo got up to push the loaded trolley out of the dining room for her. When he returned it was to wheel his father to his sitting room overlooking the spacious garden.

Angie followed and was about to make herself comfortable in an armchair when Pablo returned from the window. 'No point in sitting down,' he said. 'The Bristows will be here on the dot if I know anything about them. If you don't mind, Dad, Angie and I'll cut and run before they arrive.'

'Coward!' Bron had come into the room with coffee just in time to hear this speech. 'Still, never mind, you young ones slip away. I'll come across and let you know when the coast's clear again. I don't suppose they'll stop very late. They never do.'

Angie and Pablo needed no second bidding to go across to the barn, and Pablo switched on the percolator. 'It will have to be black,' he remarked as he turned back to Angie. 'I completely forgot to ask Bron for some milk. Do you mind?'

Angie shook her head. All the way from the house she had been half anticipating and half dreading the tête-à-tête which she knew loomed ahead of her, knowing it would be impossible to carry on a conversation for long without Robinetta's name cropping up. She bravely decided to fire the first shot, and as Pablo leaned down in a now familiar stance, his hands on the arms of her chair to say confidentially, a smile in his brown eyes, 'Do you realise it's four whole days since I saw you, Princess?' she nodded briefly as she answered,

'Yes, I know. How is it you haven't brought Robinetta down with you for the week-end?'

There was an immediate and telling silence as Pablo straightened himself and stood looking down at her, the smile quite gone from his eyes. 'Any reason why I should?' he asked, and his tones were hard.

Angie glanced away. It was going to be even more difficult than she had feared. She watched as he walked away and stood, his back turned, looking out of the window at the darkening garden. The silence stretched on and Angie couldn't think how to break it.

She was shaken when Pablo spoke because he seemed to have dismissed the subject uppermost in her mind. 'Did Richards say when you could go back to London?'

'I'm fit to go any time,' she told him. 'As a matter of fact I had intended to go to-morrow, but Bron and your father asked me to stay over the week-end, so I'm travelling back on Monday morning.' There was no reply to this and as he was still standing with his back to her Angie was unable to read his expression.

'You know what's the matter with you, my girl,' he remarked suddenly, and turned. 'Inhibitions!' Angie felt surprise stealing through her at the sudden accusation, and it must have shown on her face as Pablo walked back across the room towards her saying as he did so, 'You're one mass of them, my dear girl. I never saw two sisters more unalike. You're all wrapped up inside and Robinetta's just the opposite. An extrovert of extroverts without a selfconscious bone in her whole body. Why aren't you a little more like her?'

Angie flushed. She had soon learned as a child what a disappointment her lack of beauty had been to her mother, but this was the first time anyone had accused her of being an introvert. 'I'm not like that at all,' she burst out at last defiantly, but Pablo stopped her with,

'Well, at least you are with me. You hold back all the time. It's my opinion you're afraid.'

This time Angie was genuinely surprised. 'Afraid? What of?'

'Yourself mainly, and I imagine of your feelings for me. For you aren't so indifferent as you'd like to be, are you, Angie?'

There was silence for a moment as Angie thought this over and then she looked up and there was defiance in her eyes. 'Of course I find you attractive. I'm not good at hiding things and I must have made it pretty obvious how I felt about you before Robinetta arrived last week-end. But you don't think I'm pleased with myself for having come between my only sister and her boy-friend, do you? Can you blame me for holding back? For fighting my feelings?'

'And with what object?' Pablo interrupted her. 'There's nothing between Robinetta and me except the relationship of employer and model.'

'Indeed?' Angie didn't realise how contemptuous she sounded. 'That isn't what Robinetta told me. She says you're going to marry her.'

There was dead silence for a brief moment and then to Angelina's astonishment Pablo began to laugh. 'It's a clear case then of the "best laid plans of mice and men gang aft agley!" Surely, knowing Robinetta as you must do, you can't have believed her?'

'Of course I believe her,' Angie answered. 'She's not without her faults, but Netta's no liar.'

'Probably not intentionally,' Pablo agreed, and walking across switched off the coffee percolator. 'But she lives in a fantasy world, you must realise that at least. The truth doesn't happen always to be palatable to your beautiful sister, and it's my experience she twists things to suit herself occasionally. If it had been to anybody else she'd told this preposterous tale I wouldn't even have bothered to refute it. But hear this. I'm *not* engaged to your sister and I have no intention of marrying her. Nor, may I add, have I ever tampered with her maidenly affections,' and he looked sardonically across at Angie.

'Just the same,' Angie argued, 'it makes a difference. There can't be anything between us. You must know that—it would upset her so,' and she looked up pleadingly.

Pablo was standing in front of her, a cup of steaming black coffee in his hand and she saw his face harden. 'So you intend to hand me over on a platter to your dear sister. Tied up with blue ribbons, perhaps,' he added unkindly.

Angie could feel the all too familiar flush beginning to creep up her face as he put his point of view. It was an unpleasant feeling and her temper began to rise. She put the coffee cup down on a small table beside her and said tartly, 'It's not a case of handing you over on a platter. You're not mine to hand to anybody.'

There was silence for a moment and Angie could almost hear the echo of her own words in the room, hard and defiant.

'Am I not?' Pablo asked softly. 'Quite sure about that?' and as he came across to her chair Angie noticed how his Spanish blood seemed to have the upper hand when he pulled her to her feet. Unable to stand firmly without the aid of her crutches, she could not resist the close embrace and found herself lying against his chest as he covered her face and neck with kisses. Though she forced herself to be unresponsive she could feel an almost irresistible impulse to throw her arms round his neck and respond when suddenly Pablo held her at arms' length to look searchingly into her face, while the angry glare died slowly from his eyes.

Holding herself as rigidly as possible Angie forced herself to ask coldly, 'Finished?' At her words her arms dropped and she was able to reach behind for one of her crutches. 'You're hateful!' she spat the words out, afraid of her own trembling weakness. 'I won't stay here a moment longer. As far as I'm concerned Robinetta can have you and welcome. You don't play fair,' and she marched out of the barn as quickly as she could, banging the door behind her.

But alone in her room she had time to think over all that had taken place in the barn that evening and wish she could have the half hour over again. But out of loyalty to Robinetta could she have acted any differently? Angie wondered, as wearily she began to get ready for bed. When eventually, however, she lay in the warm darkness she wept in an orgy of self-pity. If she had tried she could hardly have handled the situation more clumsily.

Out of hurt masculine pride and a wish to make her eat her words Pablo might now deliberately seek Robinetta's company. Flaunt an association under Angie's nose, knowing if he and Robinetta began to see a great deal of one another it was inevitable they would meet. There was the added problem of how Robinetta herself would react. Perhaps, however, with her usual sense of inbuilt self-preservation she would come out of it the best of the three of them.

Thinking back, Angelina now realised that Pablo's summing up was correct. Robinetta was the supreme egoist, vain and selfish, and she did live in a kind of fantasy world, although until now it had never posed a problem to Angelina's own peace of mind. She even wondered if perhaps concentrating on her own career had left her sister without the safe, wholesome background a girl of her calibre required. Although the two sisters lived together, once Robinetta was launched as a model they didn't see all that much of one another since the sisters had different interests in their leisure time.

It must have been in the small hours before Angelina eventually dropped into a heavy sleep so that the following morning she awoke to discover that her morning tea had gone cold on the table beside her bed. She was struggling up to glance at the clock when Bron Pendleton came into the room.

'Ah, you're awake at last,' she remarked as she went over to draw back the curtains. 'I'll bring you some breakfast.'

Angie had by this time seen how late she had slept and had started an apology when she was interrupted, 'That's all right. When I brought the early morning tea you were so sound asleep I thought I'd leave you to have your sleep out. Give me five minutes and I'll fetch you a bite to eat. I'm sure you must be ready for a spot of breakfast.'

A few minutes later she returned carrying a tray and Angie savoured the mouth-watering smell of freshly made coffee as Bron handed her a dressing-gown and placed the tray across her knees. 'I'm glad you slept late this morning,' Bron remarked. 'Pablo decided he must get back to London first thing and Julius has had one of his bad nights, so I've been on the go since seven o'clock. Goodness knows why Pablo had to set off this morning. I quite thought he intended staying until Sunday night.'

Angie could have told her why Pablo had changed his plans, but she remained silent as she poured her coffee. She was relieved when Bron excused herself and hurried away, because all appetite had fled at the news of Pablo's sudden departure, and Angelina didn't want to answer questions about lack of appetite. Later, when she was up, she could dispose of the wasted toast to spare Bron a disappointment.

The week-end passed quietly. Christine Casement was having two days off, so on Sunday morning they all breakfasted late on the verandah outside Julius Pendleton's sitting room in warm sunshine. Gordon appeared in a dressing-gown looking heavy-eyed as he admitted that a party the night before had lasted later than he had expected. He yawned as he sat down and his father looked over the top of the newspaper he was reading. 'I heard you come in. A good do, was it?'

'Not bad at all. That reminds me—I've asked Marg and Alan Prior and the Fitzpatricks in for drinks this evening. Is that all right with you, Bron?'

His stepmother nodded, 'Of course it's all right. That reminds me, Marg Prior promised me the recipe for her cucumber soup when she was here last time. I'll ring later and remind her to bring it.' She got up with the words and went indoors to fetch a fresh supply of coffee and when she returned, the four of them sat on round the breakfast table reading the Sunday papers until at last Bron sighed and getting up said, 'Well, that was all very pleasant, but if we're having guests this evening, I'd better get on.'

'Don't go to a lot of trouble,' Gordon advised her as he

rose and began to help his stepmother to clear the table. 'A few bits and pieces is all they'll want. They aren't staying for a meal because I happen to know they've arranged to have dinner at the Spread Eagle at Penarwll. I've got to be in Cardiff early to-morrow, so I said I wouldn't join them. Anyway an early night isn't a bad idea,' and he yawned again as he followed Bron into the house carrying the loaded tray she had handed to him.

When they had disappeared, Julius lowered his paper. 'I hear you have arranged to go back to London in the morning,' he said to Angelina. 'We shall be sorry to lose you. Any chance of you coming to visit us when you've got rid of that?' and he pointed at Angie's plaster. 'We'd like to see you again soon. Come before the winter weather sets in.'

Angie was surprised at the invitation. Julius Pendleton had more than paid her back for her part in saving him from a nasty fall. The suggestion that she should visit them again therefore must only spring from a real desire to see her, and she was surprised at the sense of pleasure that surged through her as she stammered a halting thanks.

'A good many of my sons' friends bore me to tears,' Julius confided. 'It's a rare pleasure to meet one with a mind of her own.'

Angie mumbled an acknowledgement of the compliment, secretly wondering if Julius was referring obliquely to the situation which existed between his eldest son and herself or whether he was merely referring to the occasional involved argument on subjects of international importance which he and his guest had enjoyed during her enforced stay. Looking back, Angie could not immediately recall having displayed outstanding feats of intellectual acrobatics during their discussions, and she smiled a little warily as he continued to stare across the table.

Like Pablo, Julius Pendleton was adept at keeping his feelings hidden. Maybe he had sensed the electricity in the atmosphere when she and Pablo were together, or at least been curious about the reason behind his son's abrupt departure yesterday. It seemed, however, that Julius had no intention of keeping her in a state of apprehension for long, because suddenly he smiled and changed the subject. 'Bron tells me everything is fixed to see you to the train. I hope someone is meeting you at the other end.'

Angie wasn't aware that she expelled a sigh of relief as she replied, 'Yes, I rang Jack Bryant the other night. You met him—he's our chief photographer on the magazine.'

'Of course. Good, then that's settled. I hope the leg is soon back to normal. Pity you couldn't have stayed until it was quite better.'

At that moment Bron returned and Angie escaped to sort out her belongings. She had some difficulty in lifting her suitcases on to the bed, but managed it at last and began to fold away all except the clothes she would need for the journey. She was wearing a pretty cotton floral maxi dress which with the addition of some costume jewellery would do for this evening, so there would be no need for her to change again to meet Gordon's friends.

Since her parents' death, Angie had schooled herself to live one day at a time and had tried to keep sentimental attachment to people and places at bay, but as Bron Pendleton engaged the gears and the car began to roll down the drive the next day Angie shut her eyes for a moment so that she could not be betrayed into tears by a last glimpse of Pablo's home. Mentally, she shook herself free from a mood of near despair as Bron accelerated and the car turned into the main road and turning to her hostess, began to chatter brightly. When they had found her a seat in the train and the porter had helped her climb aboard, Bron repeated her husband's invitation to return. 'You've only to phone, Angie. Now don't forget,' she called as the train started to move, and Angie smiled and waved, knowing it was most unlikely she would ever avail herself of the invitation.

Jack Bryant was waiting at the barrier in London and came to carry her case as soon as he saw the porter helping Angelina out of the train. Half an hour later they were at the flat and Angie was being fussed over by Mrs. Wilkinson. 'It's good to be home, Wilkie,' she admitted as she hugged the motherly figure. 'Can we find Mr. Bryant some tea?'

'Not only tea. I've made one of my chocolate cakes and there's a batch of fresh scones in the oven.'

Jack, a privileged visitor, gave a shout of approval. 'Chocolate cake! Oh boy, my favourite! With walnuts, I hope, Mrs. Wilkinson.' The housekeeper nodded as she went away and Angie settled herself in a comfortable chair. 'I'll put the luggage in your bedroom,' Jack remarked, and picking up her bags he followed Mrs. Wilkinson.

Angie glanced around the room with satisfaction. It *was* nice to be home despite the warmth and hospitality she had received in Wales. Now perhaps she could stop worrying over an apparently insoluble situation and try to get back into her usual daily round, try and forget if she could the events of the last three or four weeks, and that a man had come into her life whom she found it impossible to dismiss from her thoughts. For she would have to try. He belonged to Robinetta, and she couldn't poach on her sister's preserves no matter how great the temptation. And it was going to require real determination, there was no doubt about that, for Pablo Pendleton had only to glance at her across a room to make her pulses race and her bones feel as if they were turning to melted wax. How had a normally sane, level-headed person managed to get into such a state? Angie asked herself as Mrs. Wilkinson and Jack came back into the room.

Angelina was in the kitchen watching Mrs. Wilkinson putting the last touches to supper when the sound of

Robinetta's key was heard in the lock. She came into the room like a miniature whirlwind and stopped when she saw Angie sitting at the table.

'So you're back, then,' she remarked. 'Have a good journey?' and then without waiting for an answer, spoke over her sister's head to the housekeeper. 'I can't stop for a meal, Wilkie, I've got to dash.'

'Oh, Miss Netta, and I've everything ready that you ordered this morning,' Mrs. Wilkinson complained.

'Can't help it. Something's come up unexpectedly. The managing director of Chameleon Cosmetics is giving a party and I can't miss it. I can get something to eat there.' She glanced at the clock. 'Heavens, is that the time? Pablo'll be here for me in a few minutes.' She dashed out of the room again, leaving Angie and Mrs. Wilkinson staring at one another.

A few minutes later they could hear the shower going and Angie sighed. 'Don't worry, Wilkie dear,' she said consolingly, 'I'll have to try and eat Netta's portion as well as my own.' But she knew in her heart of hearts that she had hardly appetite for one, let alone two. She would stay here in the kitchen until Pablo collected Netta, she decided, for she certainly didn't want to run into him, but when some twenty minutes later there was a ring at the bell and Mrs. Wilkinson went away to answer it a strange voice was heard asking for Robinetta.

When Mrs. Wilkinson returned Angie raised her eyebrows questioningly. 'I don't know who the young gentleman was,' Mrs. Wilkinson replied in response to the unspoken question. 'It certainly wasn't Mr. Pendleton—I know him because he's called here once or twice. Miss Netta called this gentleman Steve and she didn't seem best pleased, if you ask me,' and she walked away to fiddle with the pans on the stove for a minute or two.

'We may as well have our meal in here,' Angie said, trying not to sound as low-spirited as she felt, and getting to her feet she went over and began to collect cutlery.

'You leave that, Miss Angie.' Mrs. Wilkinson put down her wooden spoon and took the knives and forks out of Angie's hands. 'Just you sit down. I'll have everything on the table in a moment.'

In the end Angie made a good meal. Listening to Mrs. Wilkinson talking on about her various relations and trying to sort out the names and recollect what she had heard about them on previous occasions, she quite forgot her own problems and her half-formed resolution to try and have a talk with Netta this evening and get things straightened out. Later she took a book to bed and although she kept her light on until after midnight there was no sound of Robinetta's return. Finally, knowing she would have to be up early next day Angie turned out the light and settled herself for sleep.

She was in the office of *Ladies' Graces* next morning by nine-thirty, surprised by her colleagues' warm welcome when she pushed open the door and fumbled her way into the office. They all crowded round exclaiming at the suntan which she had acquired during her prolonged stay in Wales, and sympathising over the fact that she'd broken her leg. Angelina was glad she had put on a neat trouser-suit so at least her legs didn't look too unsightly and she had taken extra trouble with her make up.

Angie had been in her office about half an hour and was beginning to sort out some of the backlog of work which had been awaiting her return when the phone rang on her desk and Basil Beavis's voice boomed into her ears.

'Glad to hear you're back, my dear. Have a good journey?' And as soon as Angie had answered in the affirmative he asked, 'Think you could manage to step round to my office for a minute or two? There are one or two things I'd like to talk over now you've returned to the fold,' and he laughed at his own joke before he replaced his receiver.

A few minutes later Angie was making her way slowly along the corridor in the direction of Basil's comfortable office. He got to his feet as she pushed open the door, and coming round his desk helped her to sit down in the chair which he usually kept for important visitors.

'Glad to see you back, my dear girl. How are you feeling?' he asked. 'I got the article about Pablo Pendleton and sent him off the galley proofs this morning. I haven't heard from him yet, of course, but I expect he'll approve.'

So by this time Pablo would have received the revised article. Angie wondered whether he would consider it an improvement on the first. Suddenly Basil said, 'It wasn't as good as some of the others you've done. Find him difficult to get on with?'

'Not after the accident.'

'I see.' Basil smiled knowingly across the desk, making Angie wonder if Jack Bryant had been telling Basil what he knew of events in Llantarwyn. Basil was still talking and Angelina brought her thoughts back to what he was saying. 'If you feel well enough I'll get on to Stuart Blair. I hear he's back from Cumberland.'

Angie nodded agreement and Basil immediately turned and picked up the telephone. Ten minutes later he put the instrument down again and smiled across with satisfaction. 'Well, that's settled, then. You can go along to-day after lunch and meet him. Blair will be rehearsing some part of the week, but he says he'll fit you in between rehearsals if that's okay.'

'It will suit me fine,' said Angie, and began to get to her feet. 'I'll get hold of Jack.'

'Sit down a minute, old girl,' Basil commanded her. 'I've got something else I want to talk over with you,' and he picked up a file from his desk. 'I see you've only one more interview after Blair—the young barrister chap. Can you get them both out of the way as soon as possible, because I've had an idea for your next series. As soon as you've finished the last of the present interviews I want you and Jack to take off for the Continent. With food prices in mind particularly I think the readers might like the views of a typical housewife in all the other Common Market countries. Think you can do it? I estimate it will take about a fortnight to three weeks to get your information.'

'But I don't speak anything except Italian and a little schoolgirl French,' Angie protested.

'That won't matter,' Basil brushed aside her objection. 'Most Continentals speak English anyway, but if we happen on someone who doesn't, we can lay on an interpreter. No trouble, my dear girl. I've had John Best looking into it while you've been away and he's lining up dossiers on possibles in every capital in the Common Market countries for interviews, all of them in a similar walk of life and with about the same size of family. I want to put the whole project in one edition of the magazine, not spread out like this last series. Just little potted autobiographies, if you get what I mean, with opinions on what it's like to be in the Common Market and whether it's a good or a bad thing from their particular point of view—economy-wise mostly, of course. It's prices that are the main interest to women these days.'

Angie nodded. 'I'll see John this morning,' she said. 'Has he made any definite arrangements yet?'

'I shouldn't think so,' Basil replied. 'I assume you've got a current passport. Oh yes, I was forgetting. You've only recently come back from Venice, haven't you?' Angie nodded as she got to her feet again. 'I'll go and see John, then. It'll give me something to be getting on with before lunch.' Basil must have immediately dismissed the matter from his mind, for by the time she reached the door he was speaking on the telephone to another of his department heads.

Back in her office Angie telephoned through to her colleague. A few minutes later they were discussing the difficulties which she might encounter in her new assignment, and all the pros and cons of the proposed Common Market interviews. The first tentative plans had been discussed and approved by Angelina, and John Best had left her office when the telephone rang and she picked up the receiver to discover her old friend James Stanscombe was on the line.

'I rang through on the off-chance and was glad to hear you're back,' he said. 'How are you feeling? Well enough to come and join me for lunch?'

'I think so.' Angie was smiling as she doodled on her blotter. 'Where and when?'

They made arrangements to meet and she was freshening her make-up when the telephone rang again. Angie picked it up and answered half absentmindedly, her thoughts on the prospect of seeing James. There was no answer for a second and then Pablo's deep voice spoke in her ear. 'Stopped hating me yet?'

Angie was struck into surprised silence and it was a minute or two before she found her voice. 'Don't be absurd!'

'Now I would have thought the boot was on the other foot,' the laughing voice went on. 'However, let's argue about it over lunch. I know you don't usually like to eat at this time of day, but perhaps you could make an exception for once.'

'Sorry,' Angie refused shortly.

'What does that mean—that you won't come to lunch or you won't make an exception in my case?'

'I mean that I'm already booked.' She knew she sounded curt, but could not control the acid note in her voice.

'In that case how about dinner?'

'I'm booked for that too,' Angie lied.

'Then there's no point in continuing this profitless discussion.' The voice was hardly cordial now. 'I take it from your voice that you haven't undergone a change of heart since we last met, so I'll leave you to get ready for your date,' and the line went dead without even a goodbye from Pablo.

Angelina slowly replaced the receiver on the cradle. At least he paid her the compliment of assuming her lunch appointment was with a man. But if only he had rung ten minutes earlier, she thought sadly before turning from the telephone to meet her own reflection in the small rectangle of mirror propped against her 'in' tray. But what difference would it have made? she thought, and shrugged. It would have been foolish to meet Pablo again until she had had an opportunity to talk to Robinetta and at least clear the air between them. She must make her sister understand without any shadow of a doubt that she had no intention of poaching on Robinetta's preserves or becoming a third in a triangle with herself and Pablo Pendleton as the other two participants.

CHAPTER 5

BUT it did not appear that she would have an opportunity to do so in the immediate future. That evening she returned home to discover her sister had telephoned to say she would not be back until late, so once again Angie and Mrs. Wilkinson had supper alone, and after watching television for an hour Angie went to bed. She had only had a brief session with Stuart Blair the previous afternoon, so she presented herself promptly at ten o'clock at his London flat and was immediately engulfed in a warm family atmosphere.

He was married to a dancer, herself of some repute, and had three adorable sons, all of whom took an immediate fancy to Angie's plastered leg. They circled round her, with great interest as Stuart Blair helped her over to an armchair in the big spacious living room. 'Mind they don't trip over it,' he warned her, and turned to wag his finger at the three small enquiring faces. 'Now I know Miss Snow's leg is an object of curiosity to you three chaps, but mind what you do,' he ordered them. 'It has to be treated with great care,' and the three faces immediately turned in the direction of their father's.

Angie hastily smothered a laugh. They were of different ages but all so alike they looked as if they had been turned out of a sausage machine, and since they were all dressed in identical outfits it made their resemblance to one another more pronounced. At that moment Stuart Blair's wife came in carrying a tray bearing three mugs of milk, three cups and saucers and an enormous coffee pot. She walked with the light grace of a born dancer and when Stuart introduced her immediately sat down and started chatting away uninhibitedly to Angelina, as if she had known her for years. They found they had a good deal in common and had once even attended the same dancing school, though they had never actually met. Brena Blair, Angie guessed, must be older than herself, because the oldest child looked to be about nine or ten.

When coffee and milk had been consumed Brena picked up the tray again and shooed her three small sons out of the room ahead of her. 'I'll leave you two to get on with the work in hand,' she remarked, 'but I'll be back later. You will stay to lunch?' she asked Angie.

'Thanks, I'd like to,' Angelina accepted gratefully. It would save her having to go out and find a nearby café and then return in the afternoon—not easy when one had to drag oneself around on crutches.

The interview went well right from the very start and Angelina knew it would not take half the time nor produce the complications which had accompanied her last involved study. No probing was needed with this open, warm-hearted man, who obviously enjoyed a relaxed relationship with his wife, for when she was in the room he teased her unmercifully. Brena seemed to take this with as much good humour as her husband exuded, even drawing Angie from time to time into the friendly badinage.

The following day Stuart was due to start the first rehearsals of his latest television series and he asked Angie if she would like to visit the studios. 'The first day's a bit grim, but you're welcome to come if you want.'

'If you're sure I won't be in the way,' Angie accepted.

'You won't be in the way. I'm afraid you may be terribly bored, though,' Stuart said. 'The first day is always a bit of a shambles, isn't it, Brena?'

'Invariably,' Brena agreed, 'but I'll come too if you like, then if things get too much out of hand, Angie and I can creep away unnoticed.'

'That's a great idea,' Stuart nodded approval, and by the time Angie left the Blairs at five-thirty that evening she had arranged to meet them at the television studios the following morning so she could get first-hand experience of the filming of a television serial.

She was meeting James Stanscombe that evening to go to a concert, and she wondered as she hailed a taxi to take her home whether Robinetta would be back in time for them to have a talk. Since she had returned from Wales she had seen very little of her sister, and when she walked into the flat that evening it was only to discover that Robinetta had dashed home during the afternoon to pack before she left to model in a fashion show being held in Amsterdam.

Angie sighed as she went into her own bedroom and opening the wardrobe doors tried to decide what to wear, her mind still on Robinetta. What an unsatisfactory state of affairs, a tiny thought at the back of her mind seemed to say. She felt as if she was walking about in a thick black mist being pushed repeatedly off course as she tried to find her way. She pushed these unhappy thoughts away deliberately and concentrated on the thought of James. At least he was solid and uncomplicated, a nice man who only wanted to be good friends. Angie knew she would have a pleasant evening if she didn't allow disturbing thoughts to creep in.

And she did have an enjoyable evening, returning at midnight to find that Mrs. Wilkinson had gone to bed leaving a glass of cold milk and some sandwiches in her room. James had refused to come in and after seeing her to the lift had kissed her cheek and departed.

Angie got ready for bed and then sat reading a chapter of her book, slowly drinking her milk. It was very quiet in the flat, the only sound an occasional car or taxi passing in the street below. Eventually she gave a big yawn and putting the book down, turned out the light and lay down.

She wondered as she pulled the bedclothes up over her shoulders if Pablo also was in Amsterdam. She had not heard from him since that telephone call asking her to lunch. Would he repeat the invitation? Perhaps he had rung the office only to find her out, and certainly the switchboard would not tell him where she was. She must check up in the morning whether there'd been any telephone calls for her, she decided as sleep closed in.

But in the bustle next day of attending the rehearsal with Stuart and Brena Blair, Angie didn't have time for personal worries. The rehearsal, however, finished earlier than had been anticipated and Angie decided to call in at the office to pick up her mail.

It was late when she got there and most of the staff had already gone. She was looking through some papers which John Best had left for her to study when the inter-office phone buzzed. Lifting the receiver, she heard Basil's voice. 'Oh, you're still here! Good! Could you possibly spare a minute or two before you leave?'

'I'll be with you in five minutes,' Angie promised, and put down the telephone. She tidied her desk and stopped to have a wash on the way to Basil's office. Taking up a comb, she drew it swiftly through her short hair, noticing how tired she was looking. It had been a long and exhausting day because she had found the rehearsal as disorganised as Stuart had prophesied and even with Brena to bear her company all the bustle and excitement as the cast went through the first reading had made Angie's head spin and she wondered as she left the studio how Stuart Blair had the energy to stand up to it. It appeared, however, to have no visible effects on his immense vitality. He had seen her into a taxi and waved her off as if it were the beginning instead of the end of his day.

When she had re-done her face Angie went along the corridor to Basil's door and pushed it open, saying as she did so, 'You only just caught me; I was about to go home,' and then stopped as another figure rose from the chair in front of Basil's desk, and Angelina found herself staring into Pablo Pendleton's mocking brown eyes.

'Pablo came in to bring back the proofs,' Basil explained, and getting up pushed forward another chair for Angie to sit down. 'How did you leave the family?' Pablo enquired blandly as she sat down, and she knew she would have to behave circumspectly under Basil Beavis's shrewd eyes. From his opening remark Pablo obviously had not revealed his telephone call the morning of her return.

'They were all well.' She looked across at Pablo, hoping her glance was ingenuous enough to fool Basil. She couldn't resist adding, 'Your father wants me to go down again before the summer's over,' and saw the corner of Pablo's mouth quiver for an instant in appreciation of the taunt.

There was a laugh in his smooth voice as he replied, 'I hope you take him up on his invitation. You must let me know when you intend going. If I happen to have a spare date I could perhaps run you down.'

Angie felt rather ashamed of herself. He must have guessed she didn't want Basil to know there was anything between them that wasn't strictly business and she controlled a blush with some difficulty as she tried to appear composed. 'Thank you. I'll let you know. Just at the moment I'm rather tied up,' and she turned away from the teasing glance in Pablo's dark eyes to look across the desk at her boss. 'Basil has rather grand ideas about me going all over Europe to interview wives in the Common Market countries for a new series, haven't you, Basil?'

'Well, hardly a series, but the information will take some time to collect.' He sounded a little impatient and Angie looked puzzled. Was she being dense? she wondered as she glanced across to meet Basil's eyes. The moment their glances clashed Angie realised her efforts to appear detached were a waste of time. Pablo had not come here on the off-chance. He had arrived deliberately at a time when she was likely to be leaving the office and it must have been at his request that Basil had asked her to come down.

Angie felt the blood rush to her face. She pushed herself upright. 'Well, if there's nothing else you want from me I'll be getting along home.'

Immediately Pablo was on his feet and a hand came under her elbow. 'I'm going your way, I'll drop you off,' he suggested coolly. 'Thanks for letting me see the material before you go to print,' he called over his shoulder as he propelled Angelina firmly towards the door and, reluctant to make Basil even more suspicious of her activities in Wales, Angie had to appear complaisant.

When they were both seated in Pablo's car she turned to him. 'That was taking a mean advantage! You knew in front of Basil I could hardly refuse a lift in my condition.'

Pablo switched on the engine and engaged the gears. 'For goodness' sake, Princess, don't start making a lot of fuss about nothing. All he thinks is that I'm doing what any friend would do in the circumstances, see you home.'

'Are you sure?' Angie's question was in tones as impatient as his own. 'You're not going to tell me Basil asked me to come down to his office just so you could enquire about your family's health?'

Pablo gave a reluctant laugh. 'There's no use trying to pull the wool over your eyes, is there?' he asked. 'I knew perfectly well if I rang up again you'd either repeat your "No" or hang up on me, so I came along when I thought it was about time you left and suggested to Basil, very discreetly, I assure you, that he might like to get you to come along to his office instead of me having to search all over the building for yours.'

Angie was silent. This could well be the truth, she reluctantly admitted to herself, but Pablo's request had undoubtedly caused speculation and Angie was unwilling to have her relationship with this extraordinary and unpredictable man the subject of office gossip. Suddenly she noticed they were going in quite the wrong direction for her flat and asked abruptly, 'Where are you taking me?'

'To my studio, where else?' Pablo announced promptly. 'You haven't seen it yet. Surely you've time to have a drink at least?'

Angie didn't reply. She sat back in the passenger seat and gave herself up to the inevitable. She could hardly open the door and jump out, so she might as well accept the situation graciously. However, there was anything but a gracious expression on her face when Pablo finally stopped the car and helped her out.

As she steadied herself Angie noticed they were in a mews, and that Pablo having handed over her crutches was leading the way towards a door immediately to her right. It appeared to lead into what had once been the old stables and which was now Pablo's studio. There were houses on either side, also adapted she assumed from the old stable quarters, but the door now being held open had obviously only recently been painted and the whole premises bore signs of extensive alteration.

The paint on the adjoining houses was beginning to flake, but on Pablo's everything was neat and bright, obviously kept in tip-top condition. Angie suppressed a smile as she walked forward and through the door which he was holding open. There was a small vestibule with a cloakroom on one side and then a door on her right led straight into a vast studio.

There were cables and arc lights everywhere and at the far end two young men were busily employed in arranging what appeared to be a scene on a sunny beach. From the backcloth behind the two beautiful models Angie guessed they were meant to be sunning themselves on some Mediterranean shore. A man of about thirty was tinkering with some of the lighting equipment, but he got to his feet and walked towards Pablo and Angelina as soon as he heard the opening of the door.

As he came he glanced curiously towards Angie and once again she had to suppress a smile. Quite obviously she was not the usual kind of female to appear in these surroundings, and Pablo, as if he guessed her secret amusement, made the introductions quickly, adding as he cut short her acknowledgement. 'We'll be upstairs, Steve, if anyone wants me,' and putting a hand under her elbow he led Angie across to a flight of stairs leading to the upper floor. 'Think you can manage them?' he asked when they reached the foot of the staircase, 'or will you let me carry you?'

'Certainly not!' snapped Angie. 'I may be slow, but given time I can get upstairs perfectly well,' and she proceeded to prove her words. She was half-way up the staircase when the two young men glanced up at her as curiously as Steve had done a moment ago and Angie, before she looked away, saw them exchange a knowing glance. The two girls on the dais displayed no interest at all, however, and didn't even turn their immaculate heads.

The upper floor was in complete contrast to the business-like austerity below. Here every item had been chosen for its grace and comfort. There were thick carpets on the floors and when Pablo pushed open a door at the head of the stairs, Angie went in to one of the most charming rooms she had ever seen.

Apart from the muted green of the wall-to-wall carpeting colour leapt at her from every side. There was a blown-up colour photograph of what she guessed was a Paris street scene on one wall, on another two beautiful oil paintings. The three small mews windows were shaded by curtains in jewel-coloured velvet and there were bright cushions on the buttoned settee standing in front of the tiny fireplace. When he had seated her comfortably in a deep armchair Pablo asked, 'Feel like that drink now?' and at Angie's grateful nod he walked over to the trolley at the far side of the room. 'Will a glass of wine suit you?'

'Perfectly,' Angie said, determined not to ask for anything other than what was offered, though she would have preferred a long cool fruit drink. It had been very hot in the television studio where she had been watching Stuart Blair rehearse and her throat felt dry and parched.

Coming back across the room, however, Pablo put a glass into her hand, then went to lean against the wall by one of the windows. 'You're looking tired but a good deal better,' he remarked before Angie could think up anything to say. 'Getting back into harness must suit you. Incidentally, I must congratulate you on the rewrite. It's an improvement on that awful piece you produced and gave me to read ten days ago. What made you decide to scrap it?' Here was the question Angie had been anxious to avoid, but before she could think up an adequate retort Pablo went on. Perhaps he suspected she was unwilling to answer such an awkward question. 'Had words yet with your fair sister?' he asked. 'I suppose not, as I happen to know she's over in Amsterdam at the moment.'

'I quite thought you'd be there with her,' Angie countered, and looked up over the rim of her glass to meet his eyes.

Pablo smiled sardonically and sauntered over to lean in his now familiar position, a hand on either arm of her chair. 'You always like to believe the worst of me, don't you, dear girl?' he enquired, and gazed straight down into her eyes. 'Couldn't you just once give me the benefit of the doubt? I was convicted out of hand, of course, before you even met me.'

Angie flushed. Again he was putting her on the defensive, making her feel guilty at condemning him for playing around with Robinetta. 'Wouldn't you consider,' Pablo went on inexorably, 'ignoring that overworked conscience of yours and letting events just take their course?'

'I don't know what you mean,' Angie replied, feeling he had backed her into a corner.

'Oh, for goodness' sake drop the obtuse act!' Pablo straightened and his tones were impatient. 'You're a bright girl. You know perfectly well what I mean. And don't expect lengthy explanations or excuses. In any case, I hardly think you'd believe them, now would you?' and he turned to face her again as he drained his glass.

Angie took another sip of her own drink, feeling incapable of coping with the situation which had as usual quickly got out of hand. She could never win with Pablo, she decided, and she'd been a fool to accept this invitation. But then it occurred to her that she had had little choice. Pablo had intended to see her alone and his offer of a lift from the office had been made so he could bring her here instead. She could hardly get up and dash down that steep staircase, especially with an audience of five downstairs. They would certainly think it very odd indeed if she started hopping downstairs on her crutches, possibly with Pablo in hot pursuit.

He would have no qualms, she knew, about speaking his mind even in front of his studio staff. Not for him the cover-up or polite deception which made it all the more strange that he should be so chary of giving her an explanation of his precise relationship with Robinetta. Perhaps he was right, though, when he said she wouldn't believe his version of the affair. Had she really prejudged him? She glanced up to find he was watching her thoughtfully.

'I can almost see the wheels go round,' he said as her eyes met his, and smiled rather wryly. 'If you were any other girl I'd try and persuade you by other means than reasoning.'

'Make love to me, I suppose?' Angie remarked dryly.

'Something like that,' Pablo said, and grinned again. 'Or maybe I'm mistaken and you'd prefer to be persuaded that way,' and he strolled over and sat down on the arm of her chair.

Immediately Angie slithered forward and tried to get to her feet, but Pablo forestalled her by the simple expedient of getting to his own feet, picking her up in his arms and sitting down again with the two of them in the big armchair. She struggled feebly, but it was quite ineffective as Pablo merely tightened his grip and said, 'Sit still or you'll only hurt yourself.' His embrace grew closer until, beaten, Angie relaxed in his arms to glare defiantly into his face. 'You're quite the most objectionable man I've ever met,' she said, firing the first broadside, 'and what's more you don't play fair.'

'All's fair in love and war—or so I'm told,' Pablo said softly, and kissed the side of her cheek. 'Beautiful bones. I just can't get over Robinetta having a sister like you. She's all peaches and cream and dumb chocolate-box prettiness, while you're like a fabulous greyhound. You'll last for years when Robinetta's looks will have been long forgotten. She won't age well, while you, my love, will make a beautiful old lady.'

Angie pulled away as far as she was able and refused to be softened by his teasing compliments. 'You seem quite sure we'll still be acquainted in my old age,' she remarked, realising as she did so that she was playing straight into his hands.

'Want to bet on it?' Pablo asked, and immediately kissed her on her sullen mouth. 'Stop pouting, there's a good girl, it spoils the curve of those pretty lips of yours.' She was given no option, because as soon as he had made the request Pablo pulled her towards him again and his lips met hers at first gently and then passionately as the minutes passed.

Try as she would Angie couldn't prevent herself from responding, and some time later Pablo was sitting back in the chair gazing with every evidence of pleasure at the rosy-cheeked girl in his arms. 'There you are!' he announced triumphantly. 'I knew it would be better to kiss you into submission instead of starting another argument. Even you with your intelligence won't allow yourself to be reasoned with when you've worked up a hate against anyone.'

'You appear to have vast experience of the female mind,' Angelina said, determined not to be totally demoralised by this irrepressible man.

'Oh, I have,' Pablo replied promptly, and he grinned unrepentantly. 'Don't think I'm bragging, but knowledge of the devious reasoning by your sex has been rather thrust on me. Usually I'm quite happy to let a lady have the last word, it's easier and quicker that way, but in your case it's different.' Angelina kept silent, watching him warily.

'Now then,' Pablo went on, 'having accepted that you're not quite so averse to my company as you profess, how about us going out and getting some dinner? I don't know about you, but I suddenly feel ravenously hungry.'

'No, thanks,' said Angie. 'In any case, I've got a date.'

Pablo held her at arms' length as if to ascertain whether she was in fact telling him the truth. In response to his searching look, Angie nodded. 'Guides' honour. I'm due at the Festival Hall at seven-thirty.'

'Ring and say you can't make it,' she was ordered.

'Not likely! It wasn't easy to get tickets and I've no intention either of letting James down or missing to-night's concert.'

'If you're not willing to admit that at last you've met your fate nor break your date with this James, there's not much point in our sitting here arguing. I'd better take you home,' and Pablo got up with the words, still holding her easily in his arms. 'But I tell you one thing,' he nodded as he put her gently upon her feet and handed her the crutches, 'I'm not going to come running next time. When you feel like seeing me phone or better still, come over and tell me you've seen sense at last. Admit you can't live without me.'

'They'll be selling skates in hell before I do!' Angie's tones brooked no argument, but Pablo stood and looked at her, his head slightly on one side and a wicked light in his eyes.

'That sounded remarkably like a challenge,' he threw at her. 'All right. What will you bet next time we meet, you'll be calling on me?'

Angelina did not even trouble to answer. With a scornful smile, she slung her handbag over her shoulder, adjusted her crutches and set off across the room. Pablo was holding the door open by the time she reached it and from the look in his eyes she was sure he was about to make another provocative remark, but he disarmed her by saying softly, 'I'll go first, the staircase is steep. If you fall I want to be there to catch you,' and he walked past her to the stairs.

He made no attempt to see her further than the front door of the block of flats where she and Robinetta lived, and Angie, late for her concert, did not trouble to invite him in. She wondered if her sister was back from Amsterdam and if so whether she had seen Pablo hand her out of his car, but it appeared Netta was absent still, and as it was Mrs. Wilkinson's day to visit one of her married daughters, Angie had the flat to herself. She changed as quickly as she could, first phoning for a taxi. She had arranged to meet James at the concert hall and arrived only three minutes before the entertainment started, to find him pacing the foyer.

But Angie couldn't concentrate on what should have been for her an evening of delight, since the programme included one of her favourite musical works. Indeed, right in the middle of the Planets Suite she found her attention wandering. The music which should have been absorbing her became merely a background to her thoughts. She was busy instead remembering a heart-stopping expression in a certain pair of brown eyes, of the way the corners of somebody's mouth twitched when its owner was amused and how strong and firm one special pair of arms felt when they closed around her. Oh, Pablo! Angelina thought, why couldn't you have been a solicitor, a doctor or a fellow journalist, in any profession in fact not connected with her sister's career.

But recalling the times Robinetta with one smile had captivated the most hardened of male hearts, Angie sighed. Even unimpressionable James was not immune to her charm, and Angie had once been astonished to see him drawn like a magnet to her sister's side when Netta, in a fit of bored naughtiness, had deliberately set out to flirt with him during a dinner party. Until Netta marries and settles down, I don't stand much chance, Angie thought gloomily, then was brought back to her surroundings as the orchestra finished playing and applause burst like a tide around her. Hastily she joined in, afraid that James might have noticed her abstraction during the concert, but if he had remarked her lack of concentration he made no comment.

The rest of the week passed without incident. On Sunday the Blairs had invited her to dinner—a celebration, Stuart Blair informed her wickedly, of the fact that Brena had not once nagged during the past week. When she arrived, Angie found she was not the only guest, Stuart's agent, Sam Harris, and his wife were introduced, then a few minutes later there was another ring at the front door and Brena led in a tall, curly-haired man with a marked transatlantic accent.

He was, it transpired, a Canadian, his name Fergus Buchanan, and it soon became apparent from the way in which Sam Harris greeted him that he too was in the television business and apparently a man of some influence.

Seeing the obvious curiosity in Angie's eyes, Stuart laughed and said, 'Don't look so puzzled. I didn't tell you about Fergus firstly because I don't want any publicity about his visit and secondly nothing's finally settled, so for heaven's sake don't include any information you collect to-night in your article. Sam here would have my life. The fact is, Fergus has come over to try and persuade me to go and work for his company. We sold them my first series and it went down so well in Canada that the idea is to do a third set of adventures with authentic Canadian backgrounds and situations. Then I suppose you'll sell it back to us,' he quizzed the tall good-looking Canadian.

Fergus Buchanan grinned as he swirled the ice in his glass before replying in his attractive drawl, 'We'd be fools not to try, wouldn't you say? First, of course, we have to catch our man.'

'Meaning me?' Stuart laughed. 'Well, I'm easy. It's really up to Sam—and my wife, of course. What do you say to six months or so seeing Canada?' he remarked to Brena. 'You've often said you'd like to visit over there and meet those cousins of yours in Vancouver.'

The evening went by very quickly and Angie was surprised when she glanced at her watch to find it was eleven-thirty. During the course of her work she had interviewed many theatrical people and had frequently found them to be supremely egotistical and often childlike, pathetic in their self-absorption. She was surprised to find here a complete contrast.

Stuart and Brena Blair were anything but self-worshippers and set themselves to put their guests at ease and draw them out to talk about themselves. Sam Harris entertained them with stories about his clients, although he was careful to mention no names, and Fergus was soon telling them anecdotes about life on the other side of the Atlantic. Apparently he had lived all over the continent, being born by accident on Vancouver Island, where his mother was visiting her parents, and as he grew older going to universities and schools both in Canada and the United States. He had started in television as soon as he left college and worked his way to the top of the tree in a comparatively short space of time. It was from Sam Harris that Angie gleaned this last piece of information, for when it came to talking about his successes Fergus was more reticent.

The Blairs' guests left together and joined forces to share a taxi, dropping the Harrises off first on the way to Angie's flat. Fergus had insisted on seeing her safely home before he returned to his hotel, and as they drew up outside the block of flats and he helped her out she was surprised to see that he paid off the taxi before they went into the lobby.

As they went over to the lift he asked diffidently, 'I suppose you wouldn't take pity on a lone Canadian and have dinner with me to-morrow evening?'

Angie was careful not to show her surprise. Perhaps he was proffering the invitation merely because he wanted some company and knew no one else to invite, but this was no reason for refusal and Angie was surprised at the pleasure which flooded through her. She turned to thank Fergus and as she accepted added, 'I suppose you wouldn't care to come up for a drink?' Again to her surprise Fergus smiled and nodded as the lift doors slid open.

Long before they reached the door of the flat sounds of a party in progress could be heard, and Angie shrugged philosophically. From time to time Robinetta was apt to throw impromptu parties inviting anyone she happened to meet in the course of the evening. Returning from Amsterdam she was likely to have collected quite a few people on the plane as well as fellow workers from the fashion show. But Angie was distinctly surprised as she put her key into the front door and opened it to see Gordon Pendleton standing just inside the doorway of the big living room.

'What are you doing here?' she asked in surprise as Gordon strolled forward to shake her by the hand.

'I came up to have a quiet week-end with Pablo,' he said, and grinned as he nodded his head back over his shoulder. 'No one stringing along with Robinetta gets a quiet time, however!'

Angie introduced him to Fergus Buchanan and they went in to face the scene of revelry. Robinetta had certainly collected quite a few people, but only one or two of the faces were familiar to Angie and she could see that heavy inroads were being made on their modest stock of alcohol.

'Before everything runs out I'd better go and get you a drink,' she said to Fergus. 'Will whisky do? I'm afraid we've no bourbon or rye.'

He grinned. 'Just because I come from Canada it doesn't mean to say I only drink our own brands,' he remarked. 'Scotch will do very nicely, thank you.'

Seeing that Gordon was already holding a half-filled glass Angie nodded and went away. When she returned the two men were deep in conversation, but it wasn't long before Robinetta spotted their group and flitted down the room towards them. Angie watched as tucking a hand into the crook of Gordon's arm her sister looked limpidly up at Fergus Buchanan.

Netta could never resist a new face, Angie thought, looking back over the years at her sister's butterfly progress, so why had she finally made up her mind to marry Pablo? The one man, she thought to herself rather ruefully, who would have suited me down to the socks.

Hastily she threw off her abstraction. She couldn't stand here speechless while her sister gazed in silent admiration at the handsome Canadian, and quickly she introduced them to each other. Angie glanced curiously at Fergus Buchanan's face as he took the outstretched hand, waiting to see the all too familiar admiration creeping into his eyes.

But she was surprised to find that he looked more amused than admiring, staring down from his six foot two into the bewitching face raised towards him as if he had seen the same half flirtatious look many times in his career. Angie stared speculatively at him. Fergus certainly was a very virile-looking specimen of manhood. Maybe like Robinetta he rarely encountered difficulty in captivating anyone he set his heart on, but somehow he didn't strike Angie as a hardened scalp-hunter.

Robinetta fluttered her eyelashes, though she still held possessively on to Gordon's arm as she asked, 'You're not an American, are you?'

'No, north of the forty-seventh parallel!' If anything Fergus was making his attractive accent even more pronounced and Angie was smitten by the suspicion that he was playing a game with her sister instead of getting ready to bow the knee as most other men did. Seeing they were immersed with one another, she turned to meet Gordon's eye. 'Is your brother here?' she asked, and looked behind him to the clusters of people crowding the room.

Gordon shook his head. 'No, he went back to the studio at least a couple of hours ago saying he had some work he wanted to finish. I stayed on, I'll be motoring back to Llantarwyn in the morning. Why, did you want to see him?'

Angie shook her head hastily. 'No, I just thought as you were here he'd probably be somewhere about.'

Gordon grinned. 'We may be brothers, but we don't live completely in one another's pockets,' he said teasingly. 'As soon as the party looked like going on for hours Pablo quickly made his escape. He's not really much of a party man, you know.'

'No, I didn't know,' Angie said rather shortly, and turned to answer a remark which Fergus Buchanan had just addressed to her. Seeing his glass empty she suggested a refill and made it an excuse to steer him to the other end of the room.

Before Fergus left he arranged to pick her up at seven

o'clock the following evening, and knowing that this party of Robinetta's would probably continue into the small hours of the morning, Angie made her own escape and going to her bedroom she firmly shut the door and got ready for bed. But it was some time before she fell asleep. The noise from the party as well as the events of the evening kept her awake. As she rolled over on her side and closed her eyes, determined to make her mind a blank and get to sleep, she decided she would get up extra early in the morning and buttonhole Robinetta before she had to keep her appointment with the young barrister who was to be the last interviewee on her present series.

Mrs. Wilkinson brought in the early tea as usual at seven-thirty and by eight o'clock Angie was showered, dressed and ready for breakfast. She ate this in the kitchen with the housekeeper and then went along the corridor and knocked on her sister's door. There was no reply, so she opened it and going over to the window pulled back the curtains.

Robinetta gave a hollow groan and rolled over on to her back.

'What time is it?' she asked in failing tones. 'It feels like the middle of the night.'

Angie pushed a stool over beside the bed and sat down. 'Wake up, Netta, I want to talk to you. Do you realise we've hardly exchanged half a dozen words since I returned from Wales?'

'Not now,' her sister pleaded, and placed a hand on her forehead as if her head were aching. 'I've to be at Pablo's studio at ten. What time is it now?'

'About a quarter to nine. You've heaps of time.'

At that moment Mrs. Wilkinson came in carrying a tray of tea. At the sight of her Robinetta sat up and began chattering, obviously intent on keeping the housekeeper in the room as long as possible. But saying she had left something on the stove, Mrs. Wilkinson departed, and as soon as the door closed behind her, Robinetta stopped her flow of inane chatter and a sulky look settled about her beautiful mouth. Recognising this mulish look, Angie reckoned she would achieve nothing by staying, for Netta was evidently in one of her most unco-operative moods.

'Who was the fantastic man you came home with last night?' At least it wasn't to be a completely silent sulk.

'You mean Fergus Buchanan?' Angie asked, then at her sister's nod, 'He's a Canadian television producer. I met him at the Blairs'.'

'In T.V.?' There was sudden interest in Robinetta's voice. 'Important?'

'I gather so. He's here to fix up some contracts.' This was giving away no secrets and Angie saw she now had her sister's undivided attention. 'As a matter of fact he's asked me to have dinner to-night.'

'Has he? I wish you'd told me last night that he had connections.'

There was a thoughtful look on Netta's face. Now what is she planning? Angie thought as she got to her feet. 'I could hardly give you a potted biography in front of him, now could I?' she countered. 'You'd better get up if you're really got an appointment at ten. We'll have our talk another time,' she concluded, hoping she sounded sufficiently casual. For it was beginning to appear as if Robinetta was as reluctant as Pablo himself to discuss their relationship at the present time.

There was no doubt of the relief on Robinetta's face and no doubt any more that she was unwilling to discuss the progress or otherwise of the affair between herself and Pablo Pendleton. It would be a waste of time to try and make Netta be more open, for she would immediately assume that Angie was playing the older sister as she had so often had to do in the past, and it would never enter Robinetta's head that perhaps Angie's own personal happiness might be at stake if, in fact, she did manage to inveigle the elusive Pablo into marrying her.

That evening when Angie and Fergus Buchanan arrived back at the flat after seeing the latest controversial West End play and having a meal they found Robinetta curled up in a corner of the big settee in the living room. She was wearing a particularly attractive housecoat with a stand-up collar and billowing sleeves, and the rose-coloured shade on the reading lamp behind her head threw a flattering glow over the lovely face.

Had she sat there purposely anticipating their arrival? Angie wondered as she went away to ask Mrs. Wilkinson to make coffee. She was gone some five minutes and when she returned to the living room Fergus Buchanan got to his feet and came forward to help her into a chair. There was a decidedly mischievous gleam in his eye, and glancing at him Angie suspected as on the previous occasion that it held secret enjoyment at some thought running through his head, possibly brought on by some absurdity of her sister's.

When the tray of coffee arrived Robinetta got up gracefully from where she was still lying in a corner of the settee and began to pour out. Though she seldom offered to help, now Robinetta insisted her sister rested while the coffee was served, and it was so unlike her usual behaviour that Angie began to feel amusement well up inside her and glancing across the room she caught Fergus's eye.

No, she hadn't mistaken the gleam in his eyes. They shared the same thoughts; that Robinetta was behaving out of character and just a little too obviously. The pretty pose in the corner of the settee when they arrived; the play with the coffee things might have fooled most men, but it didn't fool this one. She was wasting her time if she thought she was impressing him, Angie thought to herself.

Robinetta was still chattering, making certain she was the centre of attention half an hour later when Fergus glanced at his watch and getting to his feet announced that he must be on his way. Angie got up to wish him goodnight, but it was Robinetta who led the way to the front door and held it open as he said his farewells. As the front door closed behind him Angie looked at her sister and raised her brows. 'I suppose it didn't occur to you that I might want to say goodnight to Fergus in private?' she asked, and had the satisfaction of seeing her sister's cheeks flush delicately before she turned and flounced down the corridor towards her bedroom.

'I didn't notice that he made much effort to get you to himself,' Robinetta retaliated as she reached her bedroom door. 'I thought he seemed quite glad to see me still up, and he showed no sign of missing you while you were out seeing about the coffee,' she added spitefully as she went into her bedroom and shut the door between herself and Angelina.

Once I would have felt hurt at receiving a remark like that, Angelina thought as she went along the corridor to her own bedroom, but I've learnt a lot about Robinetta in the last few weeks. She smiled to herself a little grimly as she remembered the gleam in Fergus Buchanan's eyes and felt a little ashamed to think she had been pleased at his indifference to Robinetta's charms.

Rather to her surprise he rang up again on the following Thursday morning and suggested that they repeat the theatre and dinner date. Angelina had been seen by an orthopaedic surgeon that morning and to her great relief the plaster had been removed from her leg. She would still need to use a stick for support, but the doctor assured her that the leg would soon be back to normal and he had brushed away her anxieties when she noticed the injured leg was considerably thinner than the other.

'You've not been using the muscles,' the doctor explained to her. 'As soon as you begin to walk properly again it will be as good as new,' and he began to scribble on a pad in front of him. 'Take this along to the physiotherapy department and fix up with them to show you some exercises,' he advised. 'In the meantime, don't overdo things. No running up and down stairs, for instance,' and he grinned, 'though for a day or two I don't suppose you'll feel much like it!'

Angie thanked him and went away, glad to be able to wear tights once more instead of the odd socks which she had been using to cover her bare toes. At least to-night she wouldn't have to hobble into a restaurant coping with crutches, watch the curious glances and answer the inevitable 'Had an accident, then?'

She went into the warm summer sunshine leaning on a walking stick which the hospital had lent her feeling like a new woman and already planning to go and buy herself something gay to wear by way of celebration. It had been hot and sticky in London all week and the clever up-and-coming young barrister who Angie foresaw would end up taking silk and one day become a judge had turned out to be boring as an individual.

Her article on his work had also entailed two days in court, and she had found some of the cases which he had defended not only tediously long but sometimes verging on the sordid. She had been amazed too at the type of people who filled the public benches in the courts. Most of them were not there like herself to appraise but seemed to have come out of morbid curiosity and Angie wondered at people having so little variety in their own lives that they preferred to spend all day in a stuffy courtroom listening to details of other people's tragedies. It smacked of an unhealthy state of mind, Angie thought as she said goodbye to her brilliant young barrister and left his chambers, not sorry that this interview was over at last and she could go back to the office and write up her article.

She knew John Best had now finalised arrangements for her and Jack Bryant to leave for the Continent the following week, and she would have to work hard to finish all her present commitments and get her homework done ready for the crowded itinerary which had been arranged. They were to be away at least a fortnight and it would be a crowded fortnight. As she made her way home that evening Angie couldn't help wondering if by the time she returned Robinetta would have announced her engagement, but somehow the mere idea of Pablo as a brother-in-law seemed remote. Perhaps her mind was so set against the possibility it refused to even contemplate such an unpalatable state of affairs.

But she was given little time that evening to dwell on unhappy subjects. Fergus Buchanan called for her early and she discovered that instead of the theatre they were going in a party first to have dinner and then on to a club along with Stuart and Brena Blair and two Canadian acquaintances of her host who happened to be visiting London. It was becoming a habit to go out with Fergus, Angie realised. This was the third time they had paired off since his arrival. Like James Stanscombe he seemed to expect nothing from her except the pleasure of her company, Angie mused to herself. Perhaps this is to be my role in life, the good sort who makes up the numbers and asks no questions, she thought, and grimaced inwardly.

But for all that she had an enjoyable evening, and if Fergus showed no signs of open admiration towards her he was an attentive host who saw to it that neither she nor his other guests lacked for anything. The club of which Fergus was apparently a member was one which Angie had not previously visited, but the service was good, the wine excellent and the small band of musicians had a wide repertoire to suit all tastes. The place was well patronised and Angie met several people she knew, one a colleague from the office as well as an old friend from her schooldays who was celebrating a wedding anniversary.

During dinner Angie had discovered that the Canadian television series, only an idea a week ago, was now officially fixed up and as soon as his present series was completed Stuart with his family would be sailing across the Atlantic to start a contract for Fergus Buchanan's company.

'You'll have to come over as well,' Fergus said as he turned and looked at Angie. 'I don't believe you've ever visited Canada, have you?'

'Once only when I stopped off for a couple of nights in Toronto before flying on to New York, so I didn't see much,' Angie admitted. 'It was during one of my university vacations. I can't say that I had time to get more than an impression of immense space.'

'Then you'll certainly have to visit over there again,' Stuart said, 'and then Fergus can show you around. How about it?'

Fergus nodded, his eyes twinkling as he glanced down into Angie's face. She might be unimpressed by his tall good looks, but it was certainly a boost for her ego to have Fergus treat her so courteously and seem to be so anxious to take her around during his stay in London. Unconsciously Angie warmed towards him. Nothing could have been more opposite than Pablo's usual behaviour. Her association with that gentleman seemed in retrospect to have been one long sparring match in which she usually got the worst of every argument. It was balm to a wounded spirit to go out with this charming man.

CHAPTER 6

ALL the week-end Angie was busy getting her things ready for the forthcoming trip to Europe. Mrs. Wilkinson had gone away for two days and Robinetta had left the previous afternoon to give a charity fashion display in Edinburgh. There had been no further phone calls from Pablo Pendleton, indeed no communication of any sort. True to his word, he was, it seemed, leaving her severely alone.

On Monday Angie spent the day revising and polishing the final draft of her article on the young barrister and arranging last-minute details about her new assignment. She and Jack Bryant were to leave in two days' time for their first interview in Brussels. On Tuesday as she was going through the morning mail she received a phone call from Brena Blair.

'I'm at a loose end to-day,' Brena announced after the girls exchanged greetings. 'Stuart will be in the studios all day. I'm wondering if you could meet me for a bite of lunch.'

Angie agreed and Brena suggested a small restaurant off Bond Street where they ate a light lunch and enjoyed a good gossip. As they were walking back towards Piccadilly after the meal Brena stopped abruptly. In the middle of the shop window beside her, displayed between expensive looking objets d'art, was an oil painting.

As Angie stopped to see what had attracted Brena's attention, her companion spoke in surprised tones. 'I'm right, aren't I, Angie? It is you?'

Angie was shocked into immobility as she glanced at the painting in the centre of the window. She could hardly believe her eyes. There she was, sitting in the old wing-backed chair in Pablo's studio barn, the Welsh countryside plainly visible through the window behind her and the plastered leg in plain view propped on a small stool. Pablo had painted her with her notebook in her hands in the act of writing. Angie gave a startled gasp, hoping that Brena would not notice her breathless surprise.

'When was this painted?' Brena was asking. 'It must have been done recently, because look, your leg's in plaster.'

Angie tried to make her voice sound nonchalant when she replied. 'It was done while I was in Wales. When first I broke my leg.'

'You never told me you'd been sitting for your portrait,' Brena said with evident curiosity, and Angie wondered what Brena would say if she admitted that the portrait's existence was a revelation to herself as well.

She took Brena's arm and hurried her past the shop window, hoping that she would ask no more pertinent questions about the picture or enquire as to the identity of the painter. She could hardly wait to get down to Piccadilly and push Brena into a conveniently cruising taxi, hoping she did not sound too hurried in her goodbyes. Angie waited until Brena was out of sight and then flagged down another cab and gave the driver the address of Pablo's studio.

All the way there anger boiled inside her at Pablo's impudent gesture, so that Angie was out of the taxi and it was driving away before it occurred to her that it could be an embarrassing interview if she went into the studio and found it as busy as she had done on the previous visit. Pablo would certainly do nothing to save her face in front of his staff, but it was too late to think of that now, so taking her courage in both hands Angie went through the door and turning into the studio found that if anything it was even busier than on her first visit.

Rather to her surprise no one took any notice of her

arrival, and seeing that Pablo was not among the occupants of the big room Angie made her way cautiously across to the staircase and walked quietly upstairs. The fact that she had no right to intrude unannounced never occurred to her as with only a brief knock she threw open the door of the living room.

Pablo was sitting comfortably in one of the big armchairs looking through a sheaf of photographs, and he glanced up as the door opened. He made no remark not even to welcome her, but his eyes started to twinkle in the way Angie found particularly maddening.

'How dare you?' she fired at him as he continued to gaze at her in silence. 'You're without exception the most hateful man I've ever met!'

'So you've seen the painting!' Pablo got slowly to his feet and walked across the room until he was standing before her.

'Yes, and I think you're beneath contempt. How dare you paint my portrait in secret? *And* sell it to some stranger in Bond Street too and leave it there for anyone to see. What's Robinetta going to say when she hears about it? Someone is sure to tell her. You must ring up the owner of the shop and tell him to take it out of the window immediately.'

'Oh, I shall, don't worry,' Pablo agreed instantly. 'It's served its purpose.'

Angie was surprised by his immediate acquiescence but refused to be pacified. 'What do you mean by that remark?' she asked defiantly.

'Well, I did prophesy that the next time we met you'd be looking me up.'

'You don't mean to say you painted the picture and displayed it simply to make me angry enough to come over here?'

'What else?' He laughed outright. 'Knowing how your mind works I knew you'd be much too furious to work out that I'd certainly never part with a painting of you and that the minute you got to hear of its existence you'd be over here like a shot.'

Angelina gasped. He had no conscience whatsoever, it seemed. She turned on her heel and walked towards the door. 'Well, I'm glad I found out just how low you can stoop,' she snapped as she reached it. But if she hoped to see signs of remorse on Pablo's part she was disappointed. When she reached the doorway Angelina found her way blocked by his slim though immovable person.

'You surely don't think I lured you all the way here just to let you tamely slang my head off and flounce out?' he asked mockingly. 'I only allow the Robinettas of this world to get away with that. Now you're here, Princess, I intend to make the most of my opportunities, so put your handbag down and make yourself comfortable. I'm glad to see by the way that you've two good legs again,' and he gazed with exaggerated admiration at Angie's nylon-clad lower limbs, a good deal of which were on view beneath the short skirt of her navy blue linen dress.

Angelina blushed. She wasn't used to compliments and Pablo's wry tones made this particular comment sound as if he was making game of her. As she said, 'Don't be so ridiculous,' and tried to push past him to the door he startled her yet again by picking her up as he had done on a previous occasion to sit down and settle her on his lap.

She was contemplating the futility of a struggle to escape from his embrace when Pablo astonished her by leaning forward and rubbing his face affectionately against her own. 'Sorry, my darling.' Angie thought she must be dreaming, so disarming was his tone of voice. 'But you're a difficult wench to woo. What can I do to prove my honourable intentions? You seem determined to fight me no matter what I do. Tell me honestly, am I really so repulsive to you? Couldn't you like me even a little?' and he kissed her soft lips.

Angie was struck dumb and searched the warm brown eyes so near her own in a desperate attempt to assess Pablo's honesty. Certainly he hadn't the look of a man who made love indiscriminately leaving a trail of broken promises in his wake, but Robinetta for all her feather-headedness was not usually one to be taken in by a philanderer. No, it was normally she who broke off an association and flitted on regardless of the bitterness she left behind.

'Can't make up your mind, eh?' The voice had regained its usual undertones of cynicism, Angie noticed vaguely. 'Are the scruples on your own account, or has Robinetta got her "Keep off the Grass" notice still hanging round my neck?' His conjecture was so acute that Angie gasped, and as she did so Pablo laughed and kissed her parted lips. There was disappointment in his voice as he said, 'So be it, Princess. I can't fight a loyalty like yours. Senseless though I feel it to be, you're free to leave,' and getting up, he set her on her feet.

As Angie, a blur in front of her eyes, walked towards the door she kept hoping for a command to her to stay, but none came. This was the second time she had shared an armchair with Pablo and felt the strength of his arms, the warmth of his kisses. If there was never to be another, she could blame no one but herself. He had made it plain that he found her attractive, but he had been right when he guessed that her misgivings were not only out of sisterly devotion but also for her own peace of mind. Though her heart told her to trust Pablo Pendleton, everything he did and said conspired to make her do the opposite.

Ironic laughter at her ignominious departure followed her as she went down the stairs and through the studio again, wishing with all her heart that she had controlled her impulse to face Pablo over the existence of the portrait. If she had stopped for a second and used her brains she might have guessed it had been put in such a prominent shop for the sole purpose of attracting her attention. Trust Pablo to get it shown in a locality where even if she hadn't spotted it herself one of her friends or acquaintances would be sure to see it. On the way back to her office Angelina cursed herself for being so stupid, but it was too late for self-recrimination. She was to find, however, that her visit to Pablo's studio was to have unforeseen repercussions.

She was getting ready to go and have a farewell dinner with James Stanscombe before her European trip when Robinetta swept into the bedroom, saying tempestuously as she did so, 'Steve tells me that you've been to Pablo's studio—not once, but twice. He saw you there only this afternoon. I thought I warned you when we were in Wales to stay away from him!'

Angie turned from the dressing-table and gazed at her flushed, angry-looking sister. So she had been noticed after all. She was trying to think up a plausible explanation when Robinetta flung herself on the bed and dissolved in a storm of tears. 'It's bad enough Pablo being so mean, but I thought I could depend on you!'

Angie got to her feet and going over to the bed laid a hand on Netta's shaking shoulders. 'Stop it! You'll make your face blotchy.' It was the first thing she could think of calculated to dry Netta's tears.

'But why did you go to the studio?' Netta asked, and getting up she faced her sister, tears still running down her flushed cheeks.

Not even when she's crying does she make herself look ugly, Angie thought to herself as she gazed into the swimming violet eyes and wondered for perhaps the hundredth time why Robinetta should be so insistent that she had no communication whatsoever with Pablo, or for that matter why she should always meekly fall in with her sister's wishes. 'Look here, Netta, I think we ought to have this out once and for all. Why all the fuss if Pablo and I meet now and then? Is there any reason why we shouldn't be friends?'

'But you know I intend to marry him,' Netta said, and laid a pleading hand on Angie's arm. '*Please*, Angie, do help me.'

'I don't see how my keeping away from Pablo is going to help you. Surely you don't think I might influence him?'

There was a wary look in Robinetta's eyes and she didn't answer as she took a lace-edged handkerchief from the pocket of her suit and dabbed at the tears on her cheeks. 'You know you promised you'd look after me when Mummy and Daddy died,' the words broke on a sob.

Angie got to her feet and going to the dressing-table continued to make up her face. This was Netta's usual tack whenever she wanted her sister's help. Although she felt that it was unfair to herself, Angie knew she would end by agreeing to all her sister's demands if only for peace and quietness, for Robinetta was capable of creating endless scenes until she got her way. In an effort to cushion the blow after their parents died perhaps Angie had been a little too soft-hearted, a little too indulgent with her younger sister.

'I shall be away for at least a fortnight, so you don't have to bother about me seeing Pablo in the immediate future,' she said rather wearily as she got to her feet to step into her dress. 'Zip me up, please, Netta, otherwise I'm going to be late. James is coming for me at a quarter to seven.'

All the way to Belgium in the plane the following day Angie went over the conversation in her mind, and if Jack Bryant thought she was in an uncommunicative mood he didn't say so, entertaining her with comments on their fellow travellers and telling her the latest escapades of his two children in his normal cheery way. They soon reached Brussels and lost no time in settling into their hotel in the heart of the city. To-morrow morning would see them beginning the first of the interviews which they had arranged. John Best had decided that it would be wiser for them to interview two women in each of the capitals of the Common Market countries so that they could decide when they got back to London who had made the more interesting comments on the cost and standard of living in their particular community.

'They're bound to be a bit stereotyped,' John had commented, 'but with luck we can make them appear dissimilar. If you do a complete thumbnail sketch of the life of each of your women then Basil can choose for himself which he likes the best. For my own part I made a choice from as varied a collection as I could, bearing in mind the fact that all our test cases had to come from roughly the same wage bracket.'

It was Jack Bryant, always an eager gourmet, who suggested asking each of the ladies being interviewed for their favourite recipes, so that by the time Rome was reached, the last capital apart from Dublin and London itself on their itinerary, Angie had a bulging folder of notes. She was tired when she let herself into her bedroom on the night prior to their return home and her first reaction was to turn on the water for a bath. As she searched in her suitcase for a change of clothes the telephone rang.

Jack Bryant's voice came to her over the line. 'Are we going out on the town or are you too tired?' he asked.

'Would you think me dreary if I say I'd prefer to dine here?' Angie asked him in return. 'I'm feeling absolutely whacked and wouldn't say no to an early night. After all, we've got to be up bright and early to catch the plane in the morning, remember.'

'Suits me. I'd like to phone Sylvia around nine-thirty anyway, but I thought as it's our last night you might want to celebrate.'

Angie made a noise indicating revulsion. 'I think I must be getting old,' she said. 'I'm going to have a leisurely bath before I get dressed. I'll see you in the small bar downstairs in about three-quarters of an hour.'

As soon as Jack had rung off Angie went and lay in the warm scented water, wondering for perhaps the hundredth time what she would find when she returned home. Twice she had phoned through to the flat in the hope of having a word with Robinetta, but on each occasion Mrs. Wilkinson had replied, only to tell Angelina her sister was not at home.

Of Pablo Pendleton there had been no word. The only unexpected event during the trip had occurred while Angie and Jack were in Paris. Much to Angie's astonishment she had arrived back at the hotel one evening to find a message from Fergus Buchanan asking her to call him at a Paris number and when Angie phoned he suggested they meet for dinner. Jack, always an easy colleague to get on with, had grinned and said, 'Have fun. I'm going to walk round Montmartre after I've phoned Sylvia. Might even go to a strip club,' and he had given Angie a playful spank as she had turned to go and get ready for her date.

The dinner with Fergus made a refreshing change, and when he admitted that it was the first time he had visited Paris Angie said curiously, 'I'd no idea you were coming. Why didn't you say?'

'The last time we met I had no idea myself, but it seemed possible that we might be able to sell some of our French language programmes over here and I came on the offchance. I must say I'm surprised how interested they are. My co-directors will be tickled to pieces.'

'Are you going home soon?' Angie enquired. 'Will you still be in London when I get back?'

'I hope so,' said Fergus, and smiled down at her. He really was incredibly handsome, Angie thought, and she wondered why his blond good looks didn't make her heart beat just a fraction quicker. Perhaps things might have been different if she had met him before she had become so hopelessly entangled with a certain enigmatical hunk of masculinity who never failed to rob her of her self-possession every time they met.

Fergus and Angie wound up their evening by doing like most visitors to Paris and climbing the Eiffel Tower to stand in breathless silence at the beauty of Paris laid out before them like a huge fairyland. They had been leaning on the parapet looking down for some minutes when Fergus surprised her by asking, 'Do you like me, Angelina?' She turned to look at him, too astonished for a second by the unexpected remark to reply. 'After all, you don't really know much about me, apart from what I've told you, of course,' he went on, and one eyebrow quirked in almost a question mark. 'I could be stringing you along about my personal affairs, you know.'

Angie's eyes twinkled as she looked up into his face. 'That's hardly likely,' she said. 'Someone would have been sure to warn me off before now.'

Fergus leaned his elbow on the parapet beside her own. 'I'm asking for a very definite reason,' and he gazed out straight before him, intent on the view below.

Angie looked curiously at his profile. Could this be the preliminary to a proposal of marriage? she thought, and wished she hadn't been quite so easy in her manner with him, perhaps unconsciously giving him grounds for hope. But that seemed hardly likely, her saner self told her as she too gazed out in front of her at the sparkling scene below. Fergus was the most straightforward of men, she would have judged, and had he been going to propose marriage he would have come right out with it. What then lay behind this ambiguous conversation?

As she pondered he suddenly turned and smiled into her eyes. 'I just wanted you to know,' he said, and his soft drawl was more accentuated than ever, 'that I have no dubious morals and my intentions are quite honourable,' and he patted her hand in what struck her as a most unloverlike way. 'Feel like a nightcap before I take you back to your hotel?' he asked abruptly, and Angie blinked. This *was* a sudden switch, but glancing up at Fergus she decided he was perhaps a little self-conscious about what he had just confided.

In the bar and all the way back to her hotel Fergus had studiously avoided any reference to his puzzling confession of integrity, and now, here in Rome, Angie recalled the episode again to ponder what he could have meant, but the inexplicable conversation still mystified her. Angie began to towel herself. Perhaps she would ask him for an explanation if he was still in the U.K. when she got back to London. She was too bushed to-night, she decided, to fathom what Fergus could have been meaning by his ambiguous words on the subject of his morals.

As she rubbed herself dry and went to dress Angie thought whimsically to herself that the boot was usually on the other foot. Many men liked to keep up the pretence that they were the big bad wolf, capable of any misdemeanour and up to all sorts of tricks. It was unusual to find somebody bent on getting the record straight and making sure that one was under no misapprehension about his true character.

The journey home the next day was tedious and instead of arriving in London by lunchtime Jack and Angie were still waiting at Rome Airport at mid-afternoon. First their plane had developed engine trouble, then unexpected bad weather had delayed flights still more. Finally, just as they were about to embark, a small aircraft crashed at the end of the runway. Nobody was injured, but there were further delays while the salvage team removed the crashed aircraft and cleared the runway for the large jets to take off.

A free lunch hadn't made Jack and Angie feel any less frustrated, and even Jack's ebullience was beginning to wear thin by the time their flight was announced and they trailed out to the aircraft carrying their hand luggage.

'I hope Sylvia hasn't been waiting all this time at the airport,' Jack said as they strapped themselves into their seats. 'I tried to get through to her at the house, but there was no reply. She'll be hopping mad if she's been hanging about for hours.'

'She must have been told of the delays by this time,' Angie reassured him. 'Don't worry. In any case, it's not your fault and it's no use getting all worked up about it. Look, they've flashed the "fasten your seat belt" sign. Come along, Jack, snap out of it. Let's have a couple of duty-free drinks and celebrate going home to dear old Britain.'

But by the time she walked slowly into the flat that evening and flung her suitcase down on to her bed she was feeling anything but excited to be home. She would have to go into the office early next morning to start sifting the mass of information in her briefcase, and she wondered briefly if Basil would approve of the line of questioning she had followed. Suddenly she felt unutterably weary, but it was more a tiredness of the spirit than an actual bodily one, and Angie, ever honest with herself, inwardly admitted that the real cause of her low feeling was a longing to be free to see Pablo with no thought of her sister to cramp her style.

The flat was empty and she wandered into the living room and uncharacteristically poured herself a stiff brandy and soda. As she sank into an armchair, kicked off her shoes and lay back sipping at the strong spirit, 'It comes to something when you start drinking alone,' she said out loud, then laughed at her own foolishness. If anybody were to come in they would think she was half mad, she mused, watching the bubbles rise in her glass, sitting alone and talking to herself.

She had finished her drink and was washing the glass when she heard the sound of a key in the front door and Mrs. Wilkinson walked in, a welcoming smile on her face.

She seemed delighted to see Angelina back and asked

if the trip had been a success. 'Well, we saw everyone we were meant to see, if that's what you mean, Wilkie.' Angie put the glass down on the kitchen table. 'But I can't say I found it really enjoyable. I don't much like hotel rooms, not night after night when you're on a job. It's different somehow when one stays in a hotel on holiday.'

'I know what you mean.' Mrs. Wilkinson had shed her coat and was beginning her preparations for a meal. 'I'd better cook enough for Miss Netta,' she remarked as she got out the electric whisk. 'She asked this morning if you'd be back to-day and when I said yes, that you'd telephoned a couple of days ago to say you'd be back by this evening at the latest, she asked me to tell you that she'd some news for you.'

'Anything special?' Angie asked. 'I'm sure she's confided in you, Wilkie, she often does.'

'Well, sometimes, Miss Angie, and it's so exciting on this occasion she couldn't keep it to herself. However, I'm not going to tell you her secret. She'll be in herself directly,' and Mrs. Wilkinson glanced up at the clock on the kitchen wall. No sooner were the words out of her mouth than Angie heard the front door close with Robinetta's characteristic slam and then her sister's high voice calling, 'Angie, are you home yet?'

She walked out into the corridor and was immediately enveloped in a whirlwind embrace. Perfume surrounded Angelina as Robinetta kissed her enthusiastically and literally dragged her into the living room. 'Oh, I'm so glad you're back! I couldn't keep it to myself a moment longer. Of course Wilkie knows, I just had to tell her. And we bought the ring this afternoon. How do you like it?' She held out a shapely hand.

On the third finger of her sister's left hand was a beautiful and very expensive-looking diamond ring. Angie gulped, feeling as if she would choke on the lump in her throat. At last the inevitable had come about and she would have to gather all her courage to face Pablo and Robinetta's imminent marriage and pretend it was everything she had ever hoped for. If it was going to mean her future happiness Robinetta must never know what she had done, she thought as she prepared to put on the act of a lifetime. Forcing herself to smile, she reached over and kissed Robinetta's smooth cheek to say, 'I wish you both every happiness.'

'We shall have that, don't worry,' Robinetta said with confidence. 'He's got money and connections, so I shall get the chances I've missed so far. You know how ambitious I am.'

Yes, Angie knew only too well. Right from the start it had never been enough for Netta that she had got on so quickly in the fashion business, become so soon a recognised face on the covers of the shiny magazines, and she had been inordinately disappointed when turned down for a film part a year ago. But Robinetta was no actress, and with only exceptional beauty to get her by, no casting director would look at her.

She was chattering on about the engagement party which she intended to give now Angie had returned to England while Angelina pondered by what means Pablo intended to further Netta's career. He had already made her a top model. What could he be thinking of now?

Angie slept badly that night, pursued into sleep by nightmarish dreams and eventually being woken by one in which she stood clothed from head to foot in black watching Pablo and Robinetta being married. In the dream she had appalled the congregation by shouting 'Yes' when the vicar came to the part about 'anyone knowing any just cause or impediment.'

Next morning when she went into the kitchen to have breakfast Mrs. Wilkinson looked up and eyed her shrewdly. 'Didn't sleep well last night, Miss Angelina. I see you've big shadows under your eyes. Come on, sit down, I've everything ready. Perhaps a good breakfast will make you feel better.'

It wasn't a very auspicious start to the day to be told one looked decidedly under the weather, Angie thought, but she smiled at the housekeeper and pulling out a chair, sat down at the table. She had applied a greal deal of make-up in the hope that it would hide evidence of her restless, unrefreshing sleep. It seemed it had been a waste of time.

By lunchtime, however, despite stern self-control, Angie was feeling more depressed than ever. A session with Basil had lowered her self-confidence still further. He had made no mention of what she was to be given when the Common Market feature was complete, and as she returned to her own office, Angie wondered if her work was suffering from the effects of her private emotional stress. Even the revised article on Pablo she knew had not been up to her usual standards, but the following one on Stuart Blair had gone like clockwork and even the article about her bright young barrister had fallen into place fairly easily.

Perhaps, however, her personal feelings about his diamond-sharp capabilities and his apparent lack of heart had peeped through, and Basil would have spotted this instantly. She must check and double-check her Common Market interviews, Angelina thought, otherwise she might well find herself being replaced, and she quailed inwardly at the prospect of losing her interesting and challenging position on the magazine.

At that moment Maggie Barlow, the magazine's fashion editor, put her head round the door. 'Feel like a spot of lunch?' she asked briefly. 'I want to hear about your trip.'

Angelina looked up and nodded at the welcome invitation. She liked Maggie, an uncomplicated character about ten years her senior, with a stockbroker husband and two darling sons at home. She seemed to have her life well organised, Angie thought as she watched Maggie come right into her office and sit down to wait.

Over lunch Maggie eyed Angelina thoughtfully. 'You know, my dear, you look as if you could do with a pick-me-up. I'm going to see the new season's fashions after lunch. Why don't you come along? It might cheer you up.'

Angie sighed. 'I'd love to, Maggie, but I must get down to some real work. Basil's on my back to get this latest series finished as soon as possible, and quite honestly I seem to have lost my grip the last week or two.'

'What you need, my dear, is a tonic of some sort or another. Why don't you go out and buy yourself an entirely new outfit? Including a hat. It's wonderful what hats will do.'

Angie laughed. 'You know I seldom wear one, Maggie. What nonsense you talk!' But the facetious comment remained in her mind for the rest of the lunch as the two girls chattered on about various items of interest to them both, and by the time Angie returned to her office she had decided Maggie's advice was well worth taking. With Robinetta's engagement party coming up, she had a good excuse to buy a new dress. Goodness knows, she would need something to boost her morale and get her through what looked like being a very unhappy evening, so Angie put away her work on the stroke of five o'clock and took a taxi to her favourite boutique.

It didn't take long to select a dress which she thought would be the very thing for a formal summer party. It was made up in swirling silk chiffon, patterned in blue, green and brown. The salesgirl assured Angie that it might have been made for her, and when she was presented with the staggering bill Angie guessed the assistant would have been likely to say the same to anyone with more money than sense.

However, she could well afford the extravagance, and she wanted to look her best when she faced Pablo again.

CHAPTER 7

When Angelina reached home, the smell of cooking assailed her nostrils as soon as she entered the hallway, and going into the kitchen to get a cup of tea before her bath she found Mrs. Wilkinson busy, between intervals of getting supper ready, in preparing food for the engagement party. A huge ham was bubbling on the top of the electric cooker, the sizzling of roasting meat was coming from the oven and trays of vol-au-vent cases were cooling on the working surface on one side of the well-ventilated kitchen.

'I didn't know what Miss Robinetta wanted, so I used my own initiative,' Mrs. Wilkinson said as she pushed a pot of tea, a clean cup and saucer and the milk jug on to the table.

As she poured out her tea Angie looked up and smiled. 'If it's anything like your previous efforts it will be absolutely superb, so don't worry. Netta knows she can safely leave it all to you.'

Mrs. Wilkinson flushed in pleased embarrassment as she bustled away and peeped into the vegetable pans on the stove. 'Supper will be in about an hour, Miss Angelina, if that's all right. I'm afraid I'm a bit behind this evening. I didn't think the pastry would take so long.'

'Don't worry, I'm not in any hurry and I expect Netta's out as usual,' Angie said, and picking up her cup and saucer she went along to her bedroom. She lay on the bed for several minutes sipping the tea. With Netta out at least she would have the bathroom to herself, she mused, but Angelina had no sooner lowered herself into the water when there was a rattle at the door.

'Will you be long?' her sister's voice called anxiously. 'I've got to get bathed and changed in ten minutes.'

Angie sighed as getting out of the hot water she wrapped herself in a towelling bathrobe. 'I might have known,' she remarked on opening the door. 'We could do with a second bathroom,' she added wryly, but Netta was in too much of a hurry to answer, and sighing, Angie went back to her bedroom and listened to the sounds of hurried preparation and then a few minutes later the bang of the front door as Robinetta departed.

Still in her towelling bathrobe, Angelina went into the kitchen and her eyes met Mrs. Wilkinson's across the kitchen table. They both laughed simultaneously.

'Miss Netta will never change,' Mrs. Wilkinson said. 'I doubt if even marriage will alter her.'

'Oh, I don't know.' Angelina's voice was thoughtful. 'She'll calm down now the right man has come along, you'll see. And in any case,' she added rather grimly over her shoulder as she turned once again to the door, 'the man she's going to marry won't stand for any hanky-panky.'

Back in her bedroom she got dressed slowly. No, Pablo would certainly insist on being master; Netta would never twist *him* round her little finger. Physically unimpressive he certainly was, but there was steel inside, as Angelina had cause to know. He would never make a complacent husband. An affectionate one certainly, a tender lover—almost inevitably—but he would allow no woman to push him around nor dance to her piping.

It was late the following evening when Angelina arrived home and Netta was already occupying the bathroom. She had finished her work on the ladies she and Jack had met during their trip, revised carefully during the afternoon and then had taken the folder with appropriate photographs for Basil Beavis to study. To her astonishment she was on the point of leaving the magazine offices when Basil phoned through to ask her to clear up one or two queries, and it had taken over an hour of discussion before Angelina could leave. She got down to the street to find it had started to rain and consequently she had difficulty in getting a taxi.

Going into her bedroom, Angie took out her new dress and hung it on the wardrobe door. The material was unusually attractive, she mused, as kicking off her wet shoes and coat she sat down to wait for the bathroom to be free. The burning question was—would the dress really suit her, for she felt in need of something to bolster a flagging self-confidence.

Some ten minutes later, Robinetta's face appeared round the bedroom door. 'I just came to tell you I've finished in the bathroom,' she began, when her eyes alighted on Angie's new dress. 'Are you wearing this to-night?' Her tone of voice was hardly encouraging.

At Angelina's nod, her sister said quickly, 'Why didn't you let me pick you out a discarded model? Don't you think this is a bit...' Netta hesitated a moment. 'Anyway, those colours are the in thing just now,' she added quickly, then before Angie could speak she said, 'I'd better get my face on. People will be arriving before I'm ready.'

It was already seven-thirty, Angie noted, glancing at her watch, even later than she thought. Her brow furrowed as she recalled Robinetta's doubtful glance at the new dress and she studied it more carefully. It hadn't occurred to her when she tried it on, but perhaps it did look just the tiniest bit matronly; more suited to someone twice her age. The frilly stand-up collar and flowing sleeves had seemed so feminine in the shop. It's too late now, Angie thought forlornly as she turned away, and anyhow, who will notice with Netta the centre of attention?

When she went into the living room half an hour later it was already beginning to fill up, and as she caught a glimpse of the creation Robinetta had chosen, an off-the-shoulder dress in silver and white which fitted her like a second skin,

Angie knew that in her high neck and long sleeves she must look more like Robinetta's mother than her sister. The golden hair was piled on top of her sister's head and confined with a silver ribbon so that just one curling lock fell on to her bare shoulder, and apart from her engagement ring, Robinetta wore no jewellery. She scarcely requires any adornment, Angelina thought, as she looked over at her younger sister, for Netta's eyes were sparkling like sapphires and her make-up was as usual perfect.

Angelina turned away as Mrs. Wilkinson ushered in the Blairs and Fergus Buchanan, and as she walked across to greet them wondered why Robinetta should have included them in the guest list.

'I'm glad to see you're back,' said Brena, as Angie greeted her. 'Fergus told me you met in Paris.'

'Yes, we had dinner together. I'm glad he's still in London. I suppose Fergus is staying to tie up all the details about Stuart's new contract?'

For a second surprise showed in Brena's eyes. 'Oh, the contract's signed and everything else is fixed. We're off as soon as Stuart has finished here.'

'Do you mind?' Angie asked. 'It will mean quite an upheaval, I imagine.'

'Actually I'm rather pleased,' and Brena smiled. 'Strictly off the record, Stuart and I have ordered number four.'

It was a second before Angelina understood her meaning, then she smiled back into the laughing eyes looking into hers. 'I suppose you're hoping for a daughter this time.'

'I don't mind,' Brena replied. 'As long as it's a healthy baby I'll be happy. Stuart, I think, would like a girl, but it's come at just the right time since I'd intended to cancel my contracts anyway to go with Stuart.'

'So the chances are the next Blair will be born a little Canadian.'

'Could be,' Brena answered, and giggled, just as Stuart came over to hand them each a glass.

'What are you two up to?' he asked, and his eyes twinkled.

'I've just been telling Angie our news. In confidence, of course.'

'Women!' Stuart Blair rolled his eyes up to the ceiling in mock despair. 'I'll leave you to your female chit-chat, then,' and he walked away again to join Fergus who was standing beside Robinetta.

Angelina glanced round the room. More and more people were arriving. She recognised an old school friend of Robinetta's and two models who frequently came to the flat. Over by the fireplace Pablo and Gordon Pendleton were standing together, apparently absorbed in some conversation of their own. Angie hadn't noticed Pablo when she first came into the room and wondered if he had arrived while she was talking to Brena. He looked up at that moment to meet her glance and raising his glass saluted her. Even across the room Angelina could see the mockery in his eyes. She gave a slight nod in response to his sardonic gesture before excusing herself to Brena on the pretext that Mrs. Wilkinson needed help at the buffet table.

It was some half an hour later and Angelina was still behind the long table on which Mrs. Wilkinson's culinary masterpieces had been set out when Stuart Blair stepped into the centre of the room and called for silence. He was holding a glass of champagne in his hand and as soon as he saw he had everyone's attention he began to speak. 'I don't intend to make a long and boring speech,' he began. 'We all know why we're here—to drink to the happiness of Robinetta and the man of her choice. I think we should do it right now. Has everybody got a glass?' and he glanced around the crowded room. Apparently satisfied, he went on, 'Well, on behalf of us all,' and he turned to where Robinetta was standing flushed and wide-eyed, 'here's wishing you well. Robinetta and Fergus, may you have a long and happy life together.'

The plate of cold salmon which Angelina was holding

dropped to the table with a thud. What had Stuart just said? She could hardly believe her ears as she looked across at her sister. But there was no doubt about it. It was Fergus Buchanan and not Pablo who was standing with an arm round Robinetta and a very decidedly possessive look in his eyes.

Angie was motionless, her mind trying to take in the tableau across the room. So this was the reason for Fergus's cryptic comments in Paris! He hadn't been attempting in a roundabout way to propose to herself, he had been endeavouring to find out whether she thought him a suitable husband for her young and wayward sister.

She was still standing motionless, confusion going through her, when a voice from behind, a voice she had no difficulty in recognising, said in cynical tones, 'I wish you could just see your face. Now you know how mistaken loyalty like yours can be.'

Angelina could feel her hands shaking and she clenched them at her sides. It was bad enough being such a fool that she had got things back to front, but to have salt rubbed in the wound by Pablo of all people was the end. She turned around about to give him a sharp retort when she saw he was holding up a hand to silence her.

'Not here and now. It's not the time. Isn't it your place to go and lead the forefront of the congratulations? Have you tucked yourself away securely here hoping that your absence won't be noticed?'

'You're impossible!' Angelina announced as she turned away, but Pablo prevented her escape by the simple expedient of putting out a hand and closing it over her elbow.

'Too late, you've missed your chance,' and he gestured to where eager crowds had gathered round Robinetta and Fergus. Certainly there was no chance of getting near the newly engaged couple now. Angie gazed across the room, very conscious of the fingers digging into her elbow, and was torn between a desire to laugh or cry or to do both at the same moment—in fact she felt on the verge of a typically old-fashioned attack of hysterics.

As if he sensed the emotions threatening to overcome her Pablo steered Angie to the nearest door and out into the corridor. 'Is there any place where we could have a few moments' privacy?' he asked impatiently.

'I don't suppose there's anybody in the kitchen at the moment,' Angelina ventured.

'Let's go there, then, by all means,' Pablo replied at once, 'because you look as if you could do with a stiff drink.' He had picked up a bottle from the buffet table, Angelina noticed, and as soon as they got to the kitchen he poured some of the liquid into a glass and handed it to her with an unsympathetic, 'Drink that.'

She glanced rather dubiously at the contents of the glass. 'I never drink whisky,' she began, and Pablo replied tersely, 'Well, you're going to on this occasion. Get it down, my girl.'

Obediently Angelina tilted the glass and drew in a deep breath as the last powerful drop disappeared down her throat, but if she hoped the singularly large amount of alcohol she had just consumed would blur the outlines of the evening she was doomed to disappointment. If anything it made her brain clearer and she saw just how much of a fool she had made of herself. It didn't need Pablo standing there, a grim expression on his face as he stared down, to remind her that she had scarcely given him a fair deal. In order to preserve peace at home and in a mistaken attempt to protect Robinetta's interests she had been prepared to sacrifice not only her own happiness but perhaps Pablo's as well, if those attempts at gallantry which she had chosen to ignore were to be believed.

It didn't look as if he was in any too agreeable frame of mind at the moment, Angelina thought as she glanced at him. There was no sign of the tenderness which she had glimpsed from time to time in his brown eyes. He looked tense and even angry as he gazed across the kitchen table at her. But Angelina still felt too bewildered at the shock she had received, and she put a hand to her brow and sighed, 'Fergus Buchanan, of all people! I didn't even know Netta had got to know him so intimately. That's what she meant then when she said her fiancé could further her career. I do hope he knows what he's doing.'

'Don't waste your sympathy,' Pablo said, and leaned back against the working surface behind him. 'Fergus Buchanan's no fool. He may look besotted with Robinetta, but let me assure you he's under no illusions as to your sister's true character, believe me.'

At this remark, delivered in Pablo's characteristically sardonic tones, Angie began to laugh and, once started, found she couldn't stop. She leaned against the table, gusts of hysterical laughter bubbling from her lips, when suddenly she was roughly shaken and saw Pablo's face inches from her own.

'Stop that, or I'll kiss you until you do!'

At his words, Angelina's laughter abruptly ceased and she gazed into unsmiling brown eyes, her own full of tears. 'You and I have a bit of straightening out to do,' Pablo went on grimly, 'but not to-night. You're in no fit state for what I've got to say. Come and lunch at the studio to-morrow.'

Angie did not reply but merely shook her head from side to side. 'Yes, to-morrow,' Pablo insisted as he released her. 'I'll expect you at twelve-thirty. Not a minute later,' and walking out of the kitchen he left Angie to her turbulent thoughts.

After Pablo's departure the evening went by in a blur. She remembered tidying her hair and touching up her make-up, erasing the traces of tears before she returned to the living room and of Fergus saying under cover of the party's uproar, 'You *are* pleased, aren't you, Angie? I wasn't sure when I broached the matter in Paris whether you really approved of me as a brother-in-law.'

Angie pulled herself together sufficiently to smile, reach up and give the tall Canadian a chaste kiss on the cheek as she assured him he would make an ideal husband for Robinetta. Inside she was wondering what Fergus would have said had she told him the truth; that in Paris she had begun to suspect him of nursing a secret passion for herself and had totally misunderstood his meaning. He would no doubt have been vastly surprised at her mistake, Angie thought as she circulated, for he had given her no real reason to imagine he found her other than a pleasant companion to take out to dinner or a theatre.

By the time everyone left Angie felt completely exhausted, and she was not cheered by the appearance of Robinetta as she wearily prepared for bed. But her sister seemed as full of life as if it were seven o'clock in the evening instead of almost four in the morning.

'Well, what do you think? Wasn't it a marvellous party? And are you coming to Canada for the wedding? I did tell you we'll be married out there? I don't seem to have had time to have a word with you lately.'

Angie couldn't help it. She turned to face Robinetta and raised her eyebrows. 'Let's be frank. You've made no real effort to talk to me,' she began. 'To start with, what about Pablo?'

Robinetta looked genuinely surprised at the question. 'What about him?'

'Well, when I left to go on my European trip a fortnight ago,' Angie replied tartly, 'it was still Pablo who was on the mat, and I was being warned off in no uncertain terms. I return fifteen days later to find you're engaged to a totally different man.'

'Oh, that!' Robinetta shrugged off her former passion for Pablo as if it was a matter of no importance. 'I found I'd made a mistake. Fergus and I are much more suited to one another. In any case, I've always wanted to go and live in Canada or America.'

Angie didn't say this was the first she'd heard of it. She slipped a nightdress over her head and turning back the covers got into bed and made herself comfortable. 'Since you seem to have arranged everything to your satisfaction and it's rather late, may we leave the rest of the post-mortem until to-morrow?' she asked Robinetta. 'I have to be in the office by nine-thirty at the latest.'

A look of astonishment flitted across Robinetta's face. She had seldom if ever been so summarily dismissed by her usually tolerant and indulgent elder sister. 'All right,' she backed towards the door as if for once in her life she was at a loss for words. 'I'll see you to-morrow, then.'

For a couple of seconds after the door had closed, Angelina stayed completely motionless, staring into space. How typical of Robinetta, she thought. Not one word of apology or explanation for her unexpected and lightning change of heart. Perhaps that might have come had she let her sister chatter on. But no apology could compensate for the last weeks of conflict within herself as she fought her love for Pablo while endeavouring to stay loyal to her sister's wishes, now all wasted effort since Robinetta had unaccountably changed her mind and decided to marry Fergus Buchanan.

Next morning Angelina woke with a start and glanced at the clock on her bedside table to discover it was nearly eight-thirty. As she got hurriedly out of bed and went to have a sketchy wash she wondered why Mrs. Wilkinson had not appeared with the early tea. She got ready for work in record time and hurried to the kitchen.

Mrs. Wilkinson was busy at the sink clearing up the last of the dishes from last night and she glanced over her shoulder in surprise as Angelina came hastily into her spotless domain.

'I'm sorry to be so late, Wilkie,' Angie began. 'I must have slept through the alarm this morning.'

Mrs. Wilkinson began to dry her hands. 'Tea or coffee

for breakfast, Miss Angie? I looked in on you earlier, but you were so sound asleep and you looked so comfortable and peaceful, I took the tea away again. Miss Netta can sleep the clock round, but it's seldom you get much of a chance for a nice morning in bed however hard you work. I thought you'd want a lie-in after the party finishing so late.' Angie's eyebrows shot up in surprise as Mrs. Wilkinson went on, 'It's Saturday morning, remember.'

Angie pulled out a stool from under the table and sank on to it. She put her head in her hands and began to laugh. 'I must be going completely out of my mind. Is it really Saturday to-day?' she asked. 'I thought it was an ordinary weekday and I was going to be late for the office.' She looked up and met her housekeeper's smiling eyes. 'Well, anyway, Wilkie, let's have some coffee if it's ready. After all the rush I must say I could do with a cup, and I'm sure you must be a bit tired too after last night.'

Within a few minutes the two women were sitting companionably on either side of the table sipping the hot strong brew.

'I must say everything seemed to go off very well,' Mrs. Wilkinson ventured. 'I was afraid for a moment with all those extra people arriving we were going to run out of something to go with the salads. It was a good thing I decided to roast that extra turkey.'

Angie smiled faintly. She didn't want to think about the party, or the extraordinary news sprung upon her last night. She still felt desperately tired and almost wished that it really was an ordinary working day and she was due in at the offices of *Ladies' Graces*. At least it would have taken her mind off her problems. She suddenly remembered the rendezvous with Pablo for this morning, or to be more accurate his command to be at the studio for lunch. As she got up from the table and made an excuse to avoid eating breakfast she was busily making up her mind that on no account would she go near him and face his anger.

On Saturday mornings Mrs. Wilkinson always cleaned the bedrooms and changed the beds, so Angie decided to go out for a brisk walk. That way Pablo would have no means of contacting her when she didn't show up. As she went to collect her handbag she caught sight of herself in the long wall mirror. She had dressed in the first thing that came to hand this morning, a neat little blue linen suit. But if I'm going to meet Pablo it will never do, she thought, and then was struck into immobility as she realised that despite a vow not to give in to his peremptory invitation she really had every intention of keeping her luncheon date.

She met her own eyes in the mirror rather shamefacedly and let her wildest dreams run riot. Now that her sister had no further interest in Pablo there might just be a chance for her. Perhaps he had really meant all those things he had said to her and it hadn't been just a philanderer's stock-in-trade.

Angie had changed no less than four times and she felt hot and flushed by the time she was satisfied with her appearance. Robinetta was still sleeping, so at least she would be spared a further inquest on last night's engagement party before leaving to keep what would undoubtedly be a nerve-racking interview with Pablo Pendleton, for Angie felt certain he would spare her nothing. She admitted to herself that she undoubtedly deserved some of the accusations which he was sure to hurl at her, for she had treated him in a high-handed and prejudiced manner in her efforts to keep the peace at home, though at the time she had thought her actions justified. What hadn't benefited from her self-denial was her own peace of mind, she thought, as she went out into the warm sunshine.

Angelina made no effort to look for a taxi spinning out the time by going the longest way round to Pablo's studio and arriving almost a quarter of an hour late. Once again the door opened at a touch, and going through the small entrance hall she entered the at present deserted room.

In the dim light coming in through the small mews

windows it looked dusty and depressing, and she felt sick at heart as she walked across to the staircase and put her hand on the banister rail. As she did so some sixth sense made her look up. A light switch clicked and Angie found herself looking up the carpeted stairs at Pablo standing above.

To her relief this morning he appeared to be neither angry nor impatient, and she walked slowly up the staircase unable to tear her eyes away from the look in his own. When she drew level with him, however, he merely put his hand under her elbow and steered her towards the living room, saying in a most matter-of-fact way, 'If you'd been two minutes longer I was going to phone around and see where you'd got to. Perhaps you'd like a long cool drink as it's so very warm to-day,' and without waiting for agreement he lowered her gently into one of the capacious armchairs before walking over to the sideboard. While he was mixing the drinks he talked quietly about various matters which really required no acknowledgement from Angie, and she gazed at his back as he made his concoctions, a very thoughtful look in her eyes.

She wasn't aware of it, but his calm manner caused her unconsciously to relax, and by the time Pablo turned, two tall frosted tumblers in his hands, the apprehensive expression which had been in her eyes when she arrived had vanished. They emptied their glasses and Angie was beginning to feel a sense of well-being stealing over her when Pablo broached the subject uppermost in both their minds.

'And how's the delectable Robinetta this morning? Totally exhausted by last night's triumph, I don't doubt.'

Angie didn't know what to reply to this remark, but it appeared Pablo didn't expect an answer, because he continued after only the most infinitesimal pause, 'You're not upset by Robinetta annexing your latest boy-friend, I suppose?'

Of all the things Pablo might have said this was the most surprising, and Angie looked up, amazement in her eyes.

'My boy-friend? Fergus Buchanan was never *my* boy-friend. I had dinner with him a couple of times because he was at a loose end and knew hardly anybody in London apart from the Blairs.'

'I see,' Pablo said, and there was a note of genuine relief in his voice. 'For a second last night when the engagement was announced I was afraid you might be upset at losing him.'

Suddenly the funny side of the situation hit Angelina and she began to laugh. She got to her feet and walked over to where Pablo was leaning against the sideboard. She put her glass down and turned to face him. 'And what about you? Are you brokenhearted at Robinetta getting herself engaged to Fergus?'

Pablo put his glass beside her own and when he turned to face her again his expression was grim. 'Now before you start going off on that tack,' he said. 'Let's get one thing absolutely straight. I was never, I repeat never, interested in Robinetta, except as one of the most marvellous models I've ever worked with. No matter what you put her in she looked absolutely superb. I'd have been a fool not to recognise and use her supremely photogenic face and figure. Of course,' he stuck his hands in his pockets and walked over towards the window, 'we saw a good deal of one another as a result. I've been very busy lately on one commission after another and she seemed to fit into each one of them. I imagine her fertile mind got to work and she decided that I'd be a very attractive parti to get her hooks into, especially as she's ambitious to do bigger and better things than modelling. Now, of course, I'm small fry compared with your Canadian friend. Fergus can get her seen by all the television companies, particularly the big ones in Canada and the United States, which is what she wants. Robinetta may never be a success on the big screen, but in bit parts and in television series over there she could make a bomb, you know, and probably will.'

Angie smiled faintly. She couldn't see the expression on Pablo's face because he had his back to the light, but from the sound of his voice he was no longer angry. He took his hands out of his pockets and turned to face her. 'Now we've got that straight you can come out from behind that smoke-screen of sisterly loyalty and perhaps we can be honest with each other at last.'

Angie raised her eyes and found that he was now looking very sober indeed. The tender light which she had glimpsed once or twice in his eyes was totally missing. They were neither tender nor smiling at the moment, but grimly serious.

'I fell in love with you,' he went on, 'the first minute we met when you walked into my barn. I never guessed, looking at the intelligence in your face, that you were going to behave in such an addle-pated manner, or that I'd have such difficulty in winning you over. I didn't even realise at first that you'd anything to do with the fair Robinetta, as I think you know, but when I did, it didn't take long to see the scales were going to be weighed heavily against me. I had little doubt that she would put pressure on you not to see me—am I right?' Angie nodded, too choked to speak, as Pablo went on, 'And I've little doubt with her fertile imagination Robinetta embellished our relationship out of all proportion, hence the way in which you ran like a startled rabbit every time I tried to take two steps towards you.'

Angie said nothing, looking appealingly across in silence. As if to cover his own feelings of uncertainty Pablo ran a hand through his hair and then smoothed it down again. He smiled rather sardonically, half at himself perhaps, then asked softly, 'Have you any idea what you've put me through?' and began to grin as Angie smiled apologetically. 'You really hated me for a bit, didn't you?' he asked her.

Angie nodded, and then going close put her hands flat against his chest. She still didn't speak, but gazed into the brown eyes now so near her own and watched with delight as the old tender look slowly returned and this time with an impish gleam to light their depths.

'I'm sorry, truly I am,' she said gently.

'So you ought to be, my girl.' Pablo's tones were admonitory, but his expression belied them and as he spoke his arms went round her tightly. 'As it says in Ecclesiastes, "There is a time to love and a time to hate!" Do you suppose this could be *our* time to love?'

Angie smiled into his eyes. 'To think I'd live to hear the day when Pablo Pendleton quoted the Bible,' she remarked.

Pablo held her at arms' length. 'My goodness,' he sighed dramatically, and pretended to be suitably abashed, 'what a reputation that fascinating sister of yours gave me,' he remarked. 'Can you still not believe me when I tell you I adored you from the moment you stepped into my life?'

For answer Angie stepped nearer and wound her arms around his neck. 'What do you think?' she asked, and held up willing lips.

'I think,' Pablo said, and now his eyes were serious again, 'that you're a teasing young monkey and in your own way almost as much a minx as your fair sister. However, there's a difference. I'm going to make sure that legally I have the right to beat you every Friday night. Regularly!'

Angie chuckled and kissed him first on one cheek and then on the other. 'You'll drag me to the altar by my hair if necessary, I suppose,' she asked, and kissed him on the tip of his nose.

'Certainly, if that's the only way I can get you there,' Pablo promised, and then his arms tightened into steel bands. 'Stop tickling me, Princess. I can stand no more provocation,' and putting up one hand he took her firmly by the chin. 'Decided then, is it?' he asked, and kissed her quickly on her lips. 'We'll go out straight after lunch and get a special licence. Agreed? I intend to tie you up as quickly as possible before Robinetta can do anything else to throw a spanner in the works. And then if you're a very good girl I might allow you to go to Canada next month to attend her wedding. In fact,' he said, looking suspiciously innocent, 'I might even arrange things so I can take you myself. How about it?'

Angelina kept him in suspense until the silence had lengthened to such an extent that Pablo's teasing turned to anxiety and he shook her gently. 'I'm willing if you are,' she answered swiftly. 'We've wasted a lot of time already. Of course everyone will say I've caught you on the rebound,' she finished.

'Everyone except my own family,' Pablo replied. 'Father and Bron guessed right from the start the effect you had on me. Why do you think Dad asked you to come back and visit them?'

Angelina looked surprised. 'I never thought of that. Did he really guess you were interested in me?'

'A downy old bird, my father,' said Pablo, and pulled her closer into his arms. 'I think once we get that special licence we'll go down to Llantarwyn and get married there, shall we? The folks will be pleased, and you've no one in London to consider, have you?'

'Not really,' Angelina admitted. 'Only Robinetta. I wonder what she's going to say about all this.'

'Who cares?' shrugged Pablo. 'Come on, let's get some food and then the special licence. I can't wait. And suddenly I feel ravenously hungry for the first time for weeks!'

Angelina was smiling as taking her by the hand he pulled her into the corridor. She was seeing the future suddenly opening up before her. Yesterday she had been in the depths of despair, wondering how to face a future having Pablo as a brother-in-law, and all at once the dark clouds had blown away. It was almost too much to take in after weeks of fighting the loving feelings she had discovered within herself. No need to resist it any more, she thought, and her fingers tightened involuntarily upon Pablo's.

As if he sensed the thoughts going through her mind, he

turned. 'Yes, we're lucky,' he nodded. 'If you hadn't met Fergus Buchanan and introduced him to your sister I might still be wasting my time drooling over a painting.'

'The painting! Heavens, I'd almost forgotten all about it. What have you done with it?'

'What do you think? I've got it here. Where else would it be? After you found out I'd gone to all the trouble of painting a portrait and getting it displayed just to needle you into coming here, how could you go on thinking I was in love with Robinetta?'

'You'll never let me forget I was so stupidly blind, will you?' Angie asked. 'But what's all this about going to the "trouble" of painting my portrait? I thought you would consider it a labour of love,' and she peeped mischievously at him from under her lashes. 'I'd like to have a really good look at it,' she went on as Pablo laughed. 'Where is it?'

'Hanging on the wall opposite my bed where I can feast my eyes on it during my lonely hours,' he replied provocatively. 'Oh, no, you don't, Princess!' as Angie turned to push wide the bedroom door. He held her firmly by the shoulders and looked deep into her eyes. 'No peeking in my bachelor boudoir until you're fully licensed. It shall be your punishment for treating me so callously,' then as if to mitigate his decision he kissed her slowly on her willing lips.

When he finally raised his head it was several minutes later and Angie opened her eyes slowly to have the last word. 'Well, at all events,' she announced as she met his laughing eyes, 'you'll never be able to accuse me of dropping into your arms like a ripe plum.'

'No,' Pablo answered feelingly, 'a prickly pear would be more like it,' and bending his head he silenced Angelina once again in the most effective way of all.